THE
GOOD
EVIL
QUEEN

MICHAEL FRIDGEN

ARCHWAY
PUBLISHING

This is a work of fiction. All of the characters, names, incidents,
organizations, and dialogue in this novel are either the products
of the author's imagination or are used fictitiously.

Archway Publishing books may be ordered through booksellers or by contacting:

Archway Publishing
1663 Liberty Drive
Bloomington, IN 47403
www.archwaypublishing.com
844-669-3957

ISBN: 978-1-4808-9882-0 (sc)
ISBN: 978-1-4808-9881-3 (hc)
ISBN: 978-1-4808-9883-7 (e)

Library of Congress Control Number: 2020921462

Print information available on the last page.

Archway Publishing rev. date: 12/03/2020

INTRODUCTION

In 1924, Richard Loeb set out to plan the perfect crime. He was eighteen at the time. Affluent and quite handsome, Loeb had grown up in a home just a few doors down from a house that Barack and Michelle Obama would purchase in 2005. He had it all—except an accomplice.

Nathan Leopold, nineteen, also was affluent, but not as easy on the eyes. He'd met Loeb at the University of Chicago. Leopold was gay. Good-looking Loeb was not. However, Loeb frequently had sex with Leopold in exchange for his assistance.

They didn't need money. The only reason they wanted to extort money from a nearby wealthy family was to prove that they could. Both Loeb and Leopold believed that their superior intellect would enable them to avoid detection. They also didn't want to kill anyone originally, but Loeb convinced Leopold that the victim would have to be killed in an inevitable act of witness elimination.

After planning for several months and going over every detail with painstaking attention, they rented a car under the name Morton D. Ballard. They found their victim, fourteen-year-old Bobby Franks, walking home from school. He had been carefully selected months before. Loeb got Bobby into the car by stating that he wanted to look at the boy's tennis racket. Leopold was behind the wheel. Once Bobby was in the car, Loeb immediately hit him on the head several times with a chisel. There was no sexual assault committed.

Leopold and Loeb drove to a large wooded area in Indiana. They placed the body in the woods and covered it with hydrochloric acid. They made sure to pour extra acid on the face and the genital area so that nobody would suspect that the boy was Jewish. They scrubbed the rented vehicle and burned their clothes.

The two men returned home and proceeded with their well-crafted plan. They made a call to the Franks residence and demanded ransom. They instructed Mr. Franks on how to proceed with the first step of many in the process of exchanging money for Bobby. Then the supposedly perfect plan became imperfect. In the Indiana woods, a hiker found Bobby Franks and notified the authorities. The body was quickly identified. Once Bobby Franks had been discovered, Leopold and Loeb's plan for ransom was over.

Leopold and Loeb might still have gotten away with murder. But a pair of eyeglasses had been found next to the body. The glasses contained an unusual hinge that had been made by only one optician in Chicago. That optician had sold only three pairs of these glasses, one of them to Nathan Leopold. That was the end of their perfect crime.

America was shocked when Loeb's family hired Clarence Darrow, the most famous attorney in the country, to defend the men. Not only were Leopold and Loeb hated for their crime, but they also were despised for their homosexual relationship. How could Darrow defend such men when the evidence clearly pointed to them? Well, he didn't.

It had never been Darrow's intent to prove their innocence. He pushed them to plead guilty on the first day of the trial. Darrow wanted this trial to serve as a referendum against capital punishment. His only goal was to argue against a death sentence. There was no need for a jury when the trial became a sentencing hearing before a judge.

For twelve hours, Clarence Darrow told Judge Caverly about the two men and their upbringings. He cited the Bible, poetry, and the leading psychiatric studies of the time. He argued that these men had not been born this way—so if they deserved death, then so did their parents, teachers, and preachers and anyone else they'd come in contact with. Society was to blame for the actions of Leopold and Loeb.

The prosecutor, state's attorney Robert Crowe, argued that if Darrow's philosophy was correct, then no one would ever be guilty of anything.

Judge Caverly had to deliberate. The definitions of compassion, justice, understanding, and retribution were at stake.

PART I

1

LITTLE CRIME ON
THE PRAIRIE

Craig Kellerman left his car behind an abandoned farmhouse on Redwood County Road 20 as the road came into Walnut Grove, Minnesota. He'd rented the car at the Minneapolis airport and changed the plates to a set he'd stolen from a Walmart parking lot in Eden Prairie. He would replace the plates before returning the car.

It was 0.4 miles from his car to the destination. Craig was six-foot-one and weighed 180 pounds. He was in great shape for a man of forty-seven. Athletic with thick dark hair, he was a runner, ate well, and lifted weights. When he went running, he turned heads. On this night, Craig wore black jeans and a large black hoodie as he ran in the ditch along the highway. He carried a satchel of black nylon across his shoulders. His hands were covered by disposable black latex gloves. He was as dark as the night.

You are way too good for this, he told himself. *But I guess you don't start with the* Mona Lisa. *You start small.* He passed a sign welcoming him to Walnut Grove and its 811 citizens. He checked his watch—3:15 a.m. *Right on time. Two streets up and take a right.*

The town was dark and quiet. He hadn't chosen winter because of the snow and possibility for tracking. He hadn't chosen summer because the museum was open every day then. He had chosen early November. There had been little snow yet, and the museum was closed for the season. The elderly museum volunteers would be too busy with their own holiday plans to care about the locked-up museum.

In just a few minutes he was standing outside a side door to the Laura Ingalls Wilder Museum. He'd never read any of Wilder's books, but as a child of the 1970s, he'd seen *Little House on the Prairie* on television. He remembered many of the episodes, especially the really creepy ones in which clowns raped people and kids were beaten by their parents.

Those guys who broke into places years ago had it so much easier. No cameras to worry about. No motion detectors. No webcams and all that. The Wild West outlaws had it made.

He reached into his dark pants pocket and retrieved a small tool. He'd practiced with it a lot. Even though he had expected some trouble, to his surprise, the door unlocked easily. *Figures. These small-town hicks don't know their own business. Sure, they run around like they're all great and everything—talking about how they love their small town and are proud of it—but they treat their own artifacts like shit. There's no pride in this shithole, but I bet there are plenty of people around this town who swear this museum is the best museum in the country—better than anything they have in those crime-ridden cities.*

Craig entered the small museum and turned on his flashlight. He had scouted out the place once, months ago—no cameras, no motion detectors, just darkness. He walked over to a far wall and saw the precious item he was after. *It's not Abe Lincoln's hat, but it's a start. Maybe I'll get to that later. But what a bunch of idiots are running this place? No display cases. No preservation. I can't believe that I can just walk right up and take it.*

He reached over a wooden rail and grabbed a quilt that was draped over a rack on the other side. He held it in one hand and shone the flashlight on it with the other. The quilt had a white background

MICHAEL FRIDGEN

with numerous large stars pieced together for the pattern. The stars were light in color and had the overall shape of the Star of David. *So this is Laura's quilt? What was that thing that Pa used to call her in the show? Little Jug? The quilt looks sort of Jewish. I doubt the real Laura liked Jews. But there was that one episode when Nellie Oleson married that gay Jew guy. I wonder how that turned out. I should probably watch some more.* He stuffed the quilt into the satchel and turned off the flashlight.

Now the temptation began. He had anticipated this. The desire to stay inside the museum and look around was overwhelming. It wrapped around him like a cloak. Craig felt like his feet were cemented to the floor, becoming almost part of it. *What else might I find? I don't need money. But I'm not supposed to be in here, and that makes me feel intense. Shit! Get it together. This is the part that messes everyone up. Get out!*

It felt almost impossible to move. He needed to decide that he was done and ready to leave. But that would mean that it was over. Plus, on top of all this emotion, he was relishing in the pride that he'd anticipated this feeling, and now it had really come upon him. *Maybe a car will drive by and jolt me back? No, don't ruin it on this first attempt. Don't let your only conquest be of a stupid quilt.*

He moved slowly toward the door. Opening that door and locking it behind him was the most difficult thing he'd ever done; it meant that he wasn't in a place where he wasn't supposed to be anymore. But now it really was done. He moved silently with the satchel back to his car.

It wasn't until well after the new year, when he was cuddling with the quilt on his couch in Duluth, Minnesota, that he regretted not stealing more.

2

S AND M

Shaynah Williams stood outside the headquarters of the Minnesota Bureau of Criminal Apprehension in St. Paul. She was waiting for her new partner to pick her up for a field run. Out of college for just over a year, Shaynah was eager to be working outside the building for the first time. It was the middle of January and cold enough that she was tempted to go back inside. But Shaynah really wanted to call someone and share her news. She looked through her enormous purse for her phone, pulled it out, and called her fiancé.

"Hey, babe," he said in his deep voice.

"Hi," she replied. "Listen, I can't talk long. But I wanted to tell you that I get to go on a field forensic case—finally."

"Hey, you didn't think that would happen for another year at least. Good job."

"I know. I'm super excited. I'm waiting for my partner to pick me up. But I wanted to tell you that we have a bit of a drive, so I might not get home until late."

"Where are you going?" he asked.

"You know I can't tell you that."

"Just a hint."

"No. I don't want to mess this up."

"Who's your partner? Can you tell me that?"

"Yeah, this Gen Xer who everyone says is kind of crabby. Late forties. He's been around a long time. But I've learned he's gay and married, and you know I'm great with queer people, so we should get along fine."

"You are great with all people."

"I'll try to remember that if he pisses me off. Anyway, I see his car coming."

"Well, I have to go to work," he said. "I'll see you whenever. Stay warm."

"I will."

Shaynah ended the call and threw her phone back into the purse, not caring where it landed. Underneath her stylish Up North parka, she wore a white shirt, a form-fitting suit jacket, dark dress pants, and black shoes with a two-inch heel. Had she known that she was going to be traveling out into the country, she'd have brought her boots to work.

A brand-new Toyota Corolla pulled up next to her. The vehicle had the symbol of the Bureau of Criminal Apprehension on the side. The symbol was a gold shape of Minnesota with a blue star in the center of the state. Around the star was a blue triangle. Shaynah had once tried to find out what the triangle meant, but nobody at the bureau knew—not even the people whose job it was to find out what symbols mean.

When the car stopped, she opened the door. "Hi," Shaynah said as she climbed into the passenger seat. "I think we've met before. I'm Shaynah Williams. I've been here a little over—"

"I'm Mark Peterson," her new partner replied in a gruff voice. "We should get going so that we can get back."

Shaynah didn't think his voice sounded very gay at all. Without another word, he pulled the car into the road and drove away from the building.

Shaynah could not tolerate empty silence, especially with someone she'd just met. "So," she said abruptly, "how long have you worked for the BCA?"

"Too long," Mark replied without sounding ironic.

"I've worked here just over a year."

"Yes, I know. Well, this is my twenty-first year with the BCA. I started the field forensic unit about ten years ago."

"It must be rewarding to start a unit and be able to see it grow and do its purpose."

"Yeah, it's great."

Shaynah took a moment to consider Mark Peterson. Average height. White. He could stand to lose about twenty pounds, but he had a full head of the most wonderful gray hair, and it was trimmed perfectly—not too long and not too short. From how clean he looked, Shaynah finally believed that yes, he was indeed gay.

"You can call me Shaynah," she said.

"I think we should stay professional, especially in the field. I'll call you Williams."

"Ms. Williams is fine," she said.

"Williams is fine," he replied. "You can call me Peterson."

"Okay, Peterson it is. What pronoun do you use?"

"Excuse me?"

"What pronoun? You know—he, him, she, her, ze, zim?"

"What the hell are you talking about?" Mark asked. "Why would you ask that? Isn't it obvious? I'm a man."

"Oh," she replied hesitantly, "I'm sorry. It's just that I'm really good with genderqueer people, and I think it's important to ask what pronouns people prefer."

"Gender what?"

"Genderqueer. It's means—"

"I don't care what it means," he interrupted. "Now, I don't know what some jackass at the office told you, but I'm a man. I'm just a man who likes to have sex with other men. I didn't think I'd need to clarify, but I'm a he and a him. Just because I'm gay doesn't mean that I want to be a woman."

"Oh, I didn't mean it like that. I just thought—"

"And another thing—I don't like hearing that word 'queer'

thrown around like that. 'Queer' is what kids used to call each other before they beat the shit out of each other on the playground."

"I'm really sorry," Shaynah replied, quite rattled. "I think we've really gotten off on the wrong foot."

"No, we haven't. You have."

"I didn't think it would go this way. I mean, it didn't at all in my head. They said that you had a husband, and I just assumed you'd be open to talking about it. It's my mistake, and I apologize."

"I don't have a husband," Mark replied. "I have a partner, and we've been together for twenty years. But we're not married like these young gays, running around with all their rights and everything. We are just fine the way we are—two men who live together, shop together, and sleep together. Also, you are young and need to learn that things will never be the way they are in your head. This isn't a movie. This isn't *Fargo*. We're not going to come upon a string of clues and solve the damn thing. It's real life."

Shaynah sat in silence. She wanted to cry but knew it would not look good. She was really starting to hate Mark.

"Anyway," Mark said, "I'm not here to make any friends. I'm sure they told you that at the office. It's going to take almost three hours to get to Walnut Grove. Why don't you put in some headphones and catch up on your NPR true-crime podcast?"

3

THE QUILT AND
THE SHOES

Craig had planned to keep Laura Ingalls Wilder's quilt. But it sort of smelled, and when he washed it, the quilt frayed quite a bit on the edges. He thought about mailing it back to the museum in Walnut Grove, with some cash and a note telling them to buy a security system. He also thought about donating it to a used-clothing charity, but he didn't want anyone else to have it. He'd made the plan and carried it out—the quilt was his.

In the end, on a day toward the end of January, when it was still blistering cold, Craig Kellerman took the quilt to a city park right on the shore of Lake Superior. He stuffed the quilt into an iron picnic grill and lit it on fire. He grilled a hot dog over it. *What would the folks of Walnut Grove have to say to me right now? What would Pa and Ma Ingalls want to say? Poor Half-Pint is dead, and Pa's not fiddling anymore either. But I'm here having a hot dog. Damn, it's cold!*

The Miller Hill Mall sat up on a hill in Duluth, away from Lake Superior. Like all American malls, at one time it had been the center of the community, with lots of stores and the typical food court.

Now, also like all American malls with the exception of the Mall of America, it was a dump. But it was indoors and heated—two things that were welcome during the first week of February when the day's high was nine below zero.

Craig sat on a bench near what had been, at one time, a central fountain. It was now a large empty vat with lime stains on the side. But from here he could see the store where all the young guys with little money bought their expensive tennis shoes. *Lower-class guy in his twenties, any color, any size—that will do. Of course, it will be an extra benefit if he has friends with him. Whatever he buys will be what I want.*

Craig wore jeans and a red sweatshirt. He was always immaculately clean. He checked his watch often. *I'll have to leave soon, or I'll be late for the restaurant. I hope some guy wants to buy shoes soon. I guess I could come back tomorrow.*

Across the empty fountain, on the back side of an out-of-date mall directory, Craig noticed an ad for the local PBS station. The ad was promoting a show called *Daniel Tiger's Neighborhood*. A cheerful cartoon tiger wearing a red sweater smiled back at him. *Is that the same Daniel Tiger that was in* Mister Rogers' Neighborhood? *Christ, I used to love that show when I was a kid. King Friday and all of them. That Lady Elaine Fairchild was a real bitch. But I remember Daniel Tiger as being kind of depressed and scared all the time—not happy like that cartoon.*

His mind wandered back to the time when he used to watch Mr. Rogers and his Neighborhood of Make-Believe. He could still see and smell the trailer where he and his dad had lived in the northern iron city of Hibbing. *It smelled like cat piss. Probably because Dad couldn't even take care of me, let alone a cat. Why didn't we just get rid of that cat anyway?*

He remembered reclining back in his dad's chair, probably around five years old, watching television by himself all day. He always thought his dad was at work. He thought all dads must work all day and then stumble in the door smelling like crap before heading to the bathroom to puke.

Shit, didn't I get it that one time? I wasn't supposed to ever watch Mr. Rogers. Dad hated him. He said that Mr. Rogers was a faggot and child raper. I always turned the channel when I heard him coming up the outside steps. But that one time, I fell asleep, and he caught me watching it. He yelled. Christ, I thought the whole trailer park would come running to see what was going on. Of course, nobody came, and he beat the hell out of me with his belt. It was always his stupid belt. I never dared to cry. But I kind of remember feeling a little better at night when I thought about Daniel Tiger and how scared he was all the time. Maybe that Rogers knew what he was doing.

Craig pictured his dad yanking his small body from the chair, ripping off his pajama bottoms, and throwing him on the couch. He remembered the yelling and the sound of the belt buckle coming undone. But he didn't remember the pain. He didn't even think about it. *I guess it must have hurt like hell. I can't remember. Who could remember anything with Dad saying what he always said over and over again? No, think about something else.*

He desperately tried to think of something, anything, else. But the image of Daniel Tiger staring at him across the depressing fountain forced his mind back to the time in the trailer. *I don't want to hear him. But I can't help it.* He heard his dad's voice, among the slaps of the belt, saying, "God, this feels so good. Shit, this feels good. Oh God, this feels good."

Why did he always have to say those things? He was drunk, I guess. Beating me probably was the only time he was happy. But why did he have to keep saying it? Over and over? "God, this feels so good."

Dad was always nice when he was done.

Stop it, Craig. Focus on a task like the therapist said. Focus on something that needs to be done that has nothing to do with whatever triggered the memory. That's what the therapist said. Focus on Charles Lindbergh's museum. Little Falls. His first model airplane. Repeat.

Charles Lindbergh's museum. Little Falls. His first model airplane. Repeat.

He repeated the thoughts many times and then breathed a deep sigh of relief when a guy of about twenty-five walked into the shoe store. The guy's pants were hanging way down, and Craig could see the entirety of his boxer shorts. *Perfect. He's going to spend all his money on the same shoes that all his friends have so that he feels special. Those are the shoes I need for Lindbergh.*

4

SCRATCHES OF A STORY

Shaynah and Mark drove most of the way to Walnut Grove without speaking. They stopped once to use a restroom and get some coffee. Shaynah was frustrated that she didn't know how to talk to him. This had never been a problem for her before—she thought she got along with everyone. Maybe he was just having a bad day. After all, every gay person she'd met before had appreciated it when she asked for their pronoun. But every gay person she'd met before was around her age. Mark was older.

Walnut Grove was in the southwestern part of Minnesota, fifty-one miles from the South Dakota border. The farther they drove, the deeper the drifts of snow grew along the highway. It was cold and windy. Eventually, they entered Walnut Grove and drove to the Laura Ingalls Wilder Museum. Two cars were parked outside, one a Walnut Grove cop car and the other a pink Cadillac with a Mary Kay decal on the back.

"So here we are," said Mark, breaking the awkward silence. "Now this is one of those thefts that was called in by the local cop. Director Hill likes us to look around and offer advice. That's it. This isn't television, so no need to solve a murder that doesn't exist. Got it?"

"No problem," said Shaynah. At this point, she just wanted to get back to St. Paul and continue with her life.

They entered the museum through the front door and were greeted by the local cop. While Mark and the cop were exchanging cards, Shaynah looked around. There really wasn't much in the building. There was a display of Wilder's books, a bunch of photos, a recreated old kitchen, and a whole bunch of creepy dolls in a glass case. Near the door sat a sort of raised desk and an area that served as a gift shop. There were bonnets on top of bonnets for sale.

"So anyway," said the cop, "this here is Marge. She's the one that called in the theft two days ago. I thought you'd want to talk to her, so I asked her to stop by. Marge, these are the people I told you about from the Department of Criminal Apprehension over in St. Paul."

"So yeah," said Mark, "I'm Peterson, and this is Williams. Tell us what you saw when you came in here two days ago."

Shaynah thought that Marge was probably 110 years old—perhaps she had even known Laura Ingalls Wilder. Since the heat was barely on in the museum, Marge kept on her long quilted coat, snow pants, and heavy boots. It was a miracle she could move.

"Yeah," Marge began, "I stopped by on Tuesday to get the mail. I'm the president of the Walnut Grove Laura Ingalls Wilder Ladies Auxiliary, so it's my job to get the mail during the off-season. The mailman throws the mail under the front door there. There's usually not too much in it."

"When was the last time you got the mail before Tuesday?" Mark asked.

"Well, with it being the holidays and all, it was back around November. Probably not too long after Halloween. Like I said, we just don't get a lot of mail, and there's no sense in coming all the way in from the country if there's nothing to get. But anyway, on Tuesday I came in here and grabbed the envelopes in front of the door. Then I went to sort them on the counter over here. That's when something caught my eye. I noticed that something was different, but I couldn't figure what it was. I went on with the mail, and then I suddenly realized that Laura's quilt was gone.

"At first I was mad because I thought that one of the ladies must have taken it to clean it without telling me. See, that would be very bad since I'm the president and all. So I got on the phone right away and started calling. I was in here the better part of the morning. Some of the other ladies stopped by too. Nobody knew where the quilt was. That's when I called the police."

"Was there any sign of forced entry?" Mark asked.

"No," the cop replied. "Marge said that the front door was locked when she got here, and I checked the side door—also locked."

"Who all has a key for this place?" Mark asked.

"During the off-season, just me and the vice president," said Marge. "I'm certain of that. We have other keys for the ladies that work during the summer, but they are all accounted for."

"Well, I'll tell you what," said Mark. "I'm afraid to say it, but I think that this is an inside job. If there's no sign of forced entry, and if the quilt was the only thing that was taken, then someone had to know what they wanted. And they had to have a key. So I think this is a matter for the local police to …"

As he continued to talk, Shaynah wandered away. She remembered an instructor telling her that for a burglary, you should always start with the most obvious place of entry. She went over to the side door, unlocked it, and pulled it open. A wall of snow about four feet high was revealed to be pressed against the door. Any sort of footprint would be long gone since the timing window for the crime was almost three months long. She bent down to inspect the lock on the door. It was a very cheap lock, and Shaynah wondered why there hadn't been more thefts. Then she noticed a few deep scratches near the keyhole.

"I was afraid that there wouldn't be much you could do," Marge was saying as Shaynah turned her attention back into the museum.

"Yep," Mark replied, "sometimes life is just like that. It's a shame too. Laura Ingalls Wilder means something to this state, and now a piece of her is gone."

"Mark," Shaynah interrupted, "come over here and look at these marks on the lock."

Mark walked over to the door and bent down for a closer look.

"See these right here?" Shaynah said. "I've seen scratches like these on photos of locks in a book I have in my office. They look just like them. These are scratches made by a universal lock pick."

"Hey, Marge," Mark shouted, "how old is this lock?"

"I don't know," she answered. "Probably at least twenty or even thirty years."

"See," Mark said softly to Shaynah, "this is a very old lock. Those scratches could have been made by God knows what anytime over thirty years."

"Old locks are easier to pick," Shaynah whispered back. "And look at the scratches. They're clean. You can see—"

"Just stop," whispered Mark. "Don't get the old woman's gossip up. It's nothing."

Shaynah excused herself and went to wait in the car. She was not happy.

5

AN ITALIAN JOB

"Hey, Craig," said a teenager in a uniformed polo shirt and jeans, "can I switch my Friday shift with Zeke for Saturday?"

"Did you ask him?" Craig replied.

"Yep, he's fine with it. He never does anything on Friday night anyway because he's so freaky religious."

"No problem, but be nice to Zeke. You don't know what he might be going through. Also, Dylan, would you want some extra hours tonight?"

"For sure. But I've already put in eight today, so it would have to be overtime."

"That's not a problem. The supply truck is running very late, and I need someone to wait for the driver, let him in, and watch him unload."

"How long?"

"You might not get out of here until two or three in the morning. Is that okay?" Craig said.

"It's more than okay—it's great. I'll get time and a half for just sitting around and waiting for a truck?"

"Yep."

"You're the best, Craig! Let me call my mom. It won't be a problem. She knows I want the money." The young man bounded out of the manager's office, reaching in his pocket for his phone.

Craig went back to finishing the next month's schedule. *You'd think after twenty years of doing this crap, I'd get faster at it. But these damn employees all have their special problems now. But it's hard enough to get restaurant workers the way it is, so I guess I'll just have to deal with it. I just need to get through it tonight, and then I'll have a whole week for myself ... and Charles Lindbergh.*

He completed the schedule, emailed a copy to the other managers, and then printed a paper version to post. Craig was wearing the same polo shirt as the teenage worker but gray dress pants instead of jeans. He got up from the desk, walked across the small office, and turned right into the kitchen. The cook didn't look up. Craig was about to check the clean dish supply when a young girl, also in uniform, approached him.

"Craig, do we have grapes?" she asked.

"What do you mean, just regular grapes?" Craig replied.

"Yeah."

"No, we have some raisins and cranberries for the salads, but no grapes."

"Well, this mom out there is demanding a small cup of grapes for her kid. I don't know. She says that she got them here once, and now the kid wants some. I told her that I didn't think we had any, but she seems pretty convinced that we do."

"I'll handle it."

"Table fourteen. Thanks, Craig. You're the best."

Craig walked through the swinging door that led from the kitchen into the main dining room. He wouldn't have needed to be told that the problem table was number fourteen. He could tell that the family seated there was high-maintenance by the sheer number of crumbs and assorted crap they had let their kid drop all over the floor. *That kid is probably five years old, way too old to need grapes. And shit, what kind of parents let a kid throw all that food on the floor and don't clean it up? Bunch of assholes. If I ever become a serial killer, these are the people I'm going to target. What do they think this is—their kitchen? Who the hell asks for a free cup of grapes anyway?*

"Hi there," he said as he approached the table. "Lindsay tells me that you'd like some grapes, but we don't have any here. Can I bring you a cup of raisins?"

"Oh no," the mom replied as she gestured toward the kid, "he'd really like grapes. I got some here before. You know how it is. Sometimes it's the only thing he'll eat." She chuckled. The dad just sat there, looking apathetic.

"Well, we don't have any grapes right now. But I can bring some crackers or dried cranberries." *Why don't you just feed the kid some of the entire meal that he threw on the floor? That's what my dad would have done. But he wouldn't have taken me to a restaurant. He would have just scooped up the shit on the floor, brought it to me in a plastic bag, and let me have at it. If you're hungry enough, you'll eat anything.*

"Are you sure you don't have any in the back?"

"Yes, ma'am, I'm quite sure."

The mom made a noise somewhere between a sigh and a groan. Still, the dad showed no interest in the discussion.

"I guess we won't be coming back here to eat again, so you can just go now. I mean, what kind of Italian restaurant doesn't have grapes?"

This one. "I'm sorry to hear that, ma'am. I'll have Lindsay bring you your check." *Do you think I really care that you're not coming back here? You're not going to come back here and throw food all around my dining room? You're not going to make a lot of extra work for me? I'm crushed—I'll really miss your business. Too bad that I know you'll be back as soon as there's another coupon in a mailer.*

Craig walked back into the manager's office and closed the door. *What I put up with in my life, and then these people come here and treat me this way. Maybe if the dad would show some concern, his kid would eat real food and not grapes. I'd sure like to tell them a thing or two about growing up without grapes. I'd like to—*

Calm down. Therapy. Think of a task. Charles Lindbergh. Little Falls. His first model plane. It's made of cast iron and in a glass case. The museum is closed all winter. But there's snow that will leave footprints. Remember the shoes that you'd never otherwise buy.

6

A WAY TO WORK

Mark Peterson and Shaynah Williams had driven all the way from Walnut Grove to Sleepy Eye before one of them spoke. Shaynah was moderately angry and felt justified in feeling this way. Mark not only had discounted her input but also had let an obvious crime go unsolved.

"I know you're upset," said Mark as they left Sleepy Eye on Highway 14. "Let's talk it out."

"Well, of course I'm upset. You just ignored the scratches I found and dismissed the whole thing when it was an obvious burglary."

"The scratches were a good catch, and I'm impressed you found them. I have the exact universal pick that made those marks in my office. We can take a look at it when we get back."

"What?" Shaynah asked. "You admit that it was a forced entry?"

"Yes, of course. There is no way it was an inside job. Anybody who really wanted to take the quilt would have made much more of a mess to make it look like a theft. They'd have taken other things too. I knew right away it had to be some sort of weird hit. Maybe there's a market for that quilt somewhere?"

"Why did you act like it was someone on the inside? Especially in front of the woman, Margie or whatever her name was?"

"There was no sense in getting her all riled up. Look, someone broke in and took the quilt because they wanted just the quilt. But it could have occurred anytime over the course of three months. There's been probably ten snowstorms since then. If there had been a killing—well, bodies leave all kinds of clues. Even vandalism and mass burglary would have a better chance of being solved. But just one quilt? Nope. It's never going to go anywhere. We don't need Marge getting everyone in Walnut Grove scared that there's someone breaking into houses and stealing things. These small towns can be like that."

"But there are things we can do. We can search online and see if anyone is selling a quilt made by Laura Ingalls Wilder."

"Go ahead," Mark replied. "You won't find anything. A theft like this is too specific to be offered online. Whoever took it either had a buyer for it or just wanted it themselves. Case solved. There can't be too many people who even know of Laura Ingalls Wilder outside Minnesota."

"Are you kidding me?" Shaynah asked. "That show is still huge. It's on television all the time. Granted, they show it on those retro channels, but my friends and I always watched it after school."

"What show?"

"Seriously?"

"I thought she was just a children's author."

"You've never seen *Little House on the Prairie?*"

"Um, I've heard of it. That's about Laura Ingalls Wilder?"

"Uh, yes, and it's awesome. And still very popular. I can't believe you've never heard of it. You're the right age for that show."

"Are you calling me old and stereotyping me again? Just like you did with the gay stuff?"

"Yes," Shaynah replied defiantly, "I am calling you out on this. And this time I'm not going to feel bad about it. You are exactly the right age to have grown up with *Little House on the Prairie*. That's a fact and not an opinion. Did you grow up in Minnesota?"

"Yes."

"Then that's even worse. This is part of our history. Plus, you yourself told Margie that Laura Ingalls Wilder means something to the state. Why'd you say that if you didn't even know?"

"Because I was standing in a museum dedicated to her and talking to someone who gives her time to the woman's legacy. I wanted her to feel good. And her name was Marge. You need to remember that to put it in the report."

"I get to write the report?" Shaynah asked with a hint of excitement in her voice.

"You mean you want to write the report? Usually, I have to yell at you young guys to do it."

"First, I'm not a guy. I'm a woman. Second, I love writing reports! I'm really good at it. You are going to be blown away by it. I already have a photo of the quilt that I got online. I should probably include some history of Laura Ingalls Wilder."

"It's a report, not a scrapbook."

"No, you're wrong. It is a scrapbook. A good report should include visuals and artifacts. The report will be the only lasting legacy of the crime. What if someone finds the quilt in two hundred years and wants to learn what happened?"

Shaynah watched as Mark rolled his eyes. She also noticed the smallest smile form on his face.

7

ANOTHER FLIGHT

C harles Lindbergh had grown up in a 1906 home on the banks of the Mississippi River in Little Falls, Minnesota. The home and detached museum were not in the actual town but lay a mile downriver in a densely wooded area. Everything in Little Falls was named after Lindbergh, including most parks and schools.

Craig, once again in a rented car with stolen plates, drove along the dark Mississippi. It was nearing three o'clock in the morning. *At least Laura Ingalls Wilder seems like a fairly decent person, even though she doesn't get near the worldwide fame of Lindbergh. This idiot was a Nazi who believed in eugenics and fathered nine kids by raping Nazi women. But he gets all the glory. He wasn't the first person to fly solo across the Atlantic Ocean by plane; he just had the best publicity. Plus, he kidnapped and killed his own kid because the poor kid had rickets, and Charlie couldn't stand for that with his belief in eugenics. What a shithole of a person.*

When the Great River Road turned into Lindbergh Drive South, Craig turned off his lights and drove slowly. *This will be like the Wilder Museum except it has a motion detector. I need to get in and out quickly. They'll find footprints, but they won't lead to anyone who looks like me. And I'll use the universal pick again.*

He pulled the car over onto the side of the road, way into a ditch, and stopped. It was very dark—a new moon. There had been a spring thaw, and the ground was wet with mud and dirty remnants of snow. He turned off the ignition and waited in the car for a bit. It was quiet. He got out, put his satchel around his shoulder, put on his new black latex gloves, and started walking toward the museum. He knew about the motion detectors but suspected that the museum might also have a camera. He pulled a black nylon cover over his head.

Craig approached the front door. It was easier to access this door, and since there was at least some sort of security in place, he didn't think it mattered which door he chose. He grabbed the universal pick from his satchel and went to work. It wouldn't work. *Goddamn it! They have a newer lock. This wasn't here when I visited last summer. Should I abort? No, I have to have that plane. I need it too badly. I can't go back to the restaurant and face those customers without knowing that I have this prize. Shit, I will have to break the window.*

He put the lock pick back into the satchel and felt around for a glass-cutting tool. *I have been anxious to try this anyway.* The doors were made entirely of glass. Craig pressed the black round tool against the glass and started to move it in a circular manner. When he pulled it away, the tool had left a deep gouge in the glass but had not penetrated it. He did it again. This time, a circle of glass fell into the museum and crashed on the floor. He froze, waiting for an alarm. But nothing happened.

Quickly, he reached his arm through the hole in the glass and unlocked the door from the inside. Once in the museum, he moved smoothly to the exhibit room. Now, suddenly, a loud alarm sounded. He was prepared and did not even jump when it began. He confidently walked over to a wooden trunk that was sitting on the floor. The trunk was full of Lindbergh's childhood toys and was covered with glass. Craig used the same tool to cut through the glass. Since this was a glass of much lesser quality, it cut easily.

A circle of glass fell into the trunk and smashed over some toys that Craig didn't care about. He wanted Charles Lindbergh's first airplane. He knew exactly where it was, and he grabbed the small cast-iron object, threw it in the satchel, and headed toward the door. He'd accomplished all of this without the use of a flashlight.

Then, on his way out, he stopped in the doorway. He turned to look back into the museum. *I want to just stand here and breathe. I don't want to steal anything else, but I want to see how long I can make the feeling last. But this isn't Walnut Grove, with no security and lousy police. Little Falls is bigger, and they already know that there's a problem. They will assume it's a false alarm, but they will be here soon anyway. I just want it to last. But I have to go. Just go!*

Craig tore himself away from the museum's front entrance and ran toward the car. He flung the satchel onto the passenger seat and sped down Lindbergh Drive South as fast as he could. When he got to the larger road ahead, he took off his head covering, turned on his lights, and drove normally. By the time he reached Brainerd, he knew that he wouldn't be caught. He drove the two hours back to Duluth in peace.

8

PLANES CRASH

The next morning, Craig slept in late. He hadn't gotten home until almost six o'clock in the morning. He had taken a week off from work so that he could relish in the feeling of taking something that a rich and famous person had once wanted.

He got up to use the bathroom in his small two-bedroom home on the hill in Duluth. It wasn't the best part of town, but it certainly wasn't the worst. After the bathroom, he crawled back into bed. He wasn't hungry and usually skipped breakfast anyway. For a child who had grown up eating poorly, Craig as an adult had developed a healthy eating regimen that was almost obsessive. He'd eaten so many plastic-wrapped foods as a kid that the sight of them made him sick.

Craig sat in bed and played with Lindbergh's first airplane. It wasn't in great shape, with lots of worn paint and scratches. *I guess Charlie treated this plane the same way that he treated his own kid. I had a model airplane made of thin Styrofoam and paper once. I got it at the Blessed Sacrament Church festival. I remember they had some game where you put a quarter in a bucket that was attached to a rope. Then you passed the bucket over a sheet that was tied upright between two long stakes. You held on to a fishing pole until some unseen person threw the bucket back over the sheet with a prize in it. I guess it was supposed to be like fishing. Once, in my bucket there was the model airplane made of Styrofoam.*

Who took me to that festival? I think Mom had already left, and Dad would never have done it. I remember it was Blessed Sacrament Church because I walked past it on the way to high school when I was older. Was it the woman from the trailer next to ours who felt sorry for me? Maybe.

I sure loved that plane. I made it fly all over the trailer and sometimes even outside. I always kept it hidden from Dad—until one day when he came home in the truck and caught me playing with it outside. He told me that he wanted to see it. I kept it behind my back. But he said he wanted to throw it to me. I gave it to him, and he dropped it on the ground and stomped on it with his snow boots. Christ! I was so mad. But I didn't cry—nope, not at all.

I sure loved that plane. I really did. I loved watching it glide in the air. I wanted to be a pilot then. Shit, that turned out to be some sort of fairytale. Dad grabbed it and threw it in the muddy wet snow and stomped on it. I heard the thick Styrofoam crack. It was useless then.

Craig got out of bed and dressed quickly in jeans and a sweatshirt. He put on his heavy coat and boots, walked into the garage, and jumped on his bicycle. His black satchel was across his shoulder. He biked a short distance to one of the many beautiful city parks in Duluth. Congdon Park followed the edge of Tischer Creek before it flowed into Lake Superior near Glensheen, the Congdon Mansion. There were many rocks along the stream.

Craig flung his bike aside and walked down to the water. Nobody else was around. Though the creek was mostly frozen on top, a large current of fast water was running underneath the crystal clear thin ice. He took the plane out from his satchel and placed it on a large rock. With a smaller rock, he began to smash the toy over and over again.

He kept smashing and smashing until the plane was just several hunks of metal in different sizes and shapes. Then he took the small rock and bashed a hole through the ice. He pushed the iron pieces of the plane into the hole and watched them disappear in the fast creek. *Ironic. The iron that made that toy probably came from this part of Minnesota. And now it's back here again. And now nobody else will ever have Charles Lindbergh's first airplane.*

As he was walking back to his car, he paused along the creek. He didn't feel well and grabbed onto a large rock for support. *Shit, it's coming back. I didn't get much of a break this time.* A sadness rose up in his body. When it reached his brain, it made him think that he would never be happy. That's when the sadness turned into panic.

I can't wait until fall. I've got the week off, and I have to use it. Sauk Centre, Minnesota. Sinclair Lewis. Sauk Centre, Minnesota. Sinclair Lewis. Sauk …

9

A SPREE OF MINNESOTA HISTORY

Shaynah double-checked her computer in their BCA car. After confirming the information, she got out and closed the door. Mark was walking toward her while talking on his phone. The sky was gray, and spring would not come to this part of Minnesota for at least another six weeks. The road was dirty and full of so-called snirt—a mixture of snow and dirt common to rural Minnesota at this time of year. She was standing just down the road from the Charles Lindbergh Museum and Boyhood Home in Little Falls.

"Well," said Mark, "I've got some news. Director Hill just called. Do you know who Sinclair Lewis is?"

"Um," Shaynah replied, "the name sounds kind of familiar, but I'm not real sure. Isn't there a sign about him on I-94 somewhere?"

"Sauk Centre. He's actually one of the few authors that I enjoy reading. He wrote *Main Street*. He was born and raised in Sauk Centre. They have a museum for him over there."

"Oh yeah, I think I remember now. The Mainstreeters is the mascot for their high school. Didn't he win the Nobel Prize for that book? I sort of remember my English teacher mentioning that."

"He was the first American to win the Nobel Prize, but he didn't win it for *Main Street*. He won it for a book called *Babbitt*."

"Never heard of it," said Shaynah.

"I'm not surprised. He's an acquired taste. Anyway, there was a theft at his museum last night."

"No kidding!"

"Yep. Similar style. Someone just broke through the door and took the urn that held his ashes."

"Seriously? They took the poor guy's ashes?"

"No, just the urn. The ashes are buried in the Sauk Centre cemetery. But he died in Rome, and they sent the ashes back in the urn. I guess the people here dumped the ashes in the grave and put the empty urn on display."

"Someone is really out to get famous Minnesotans."

"But what did you find out from the scans you got from the Little Falls PD?" Mark asked.

"Yeah," Shaynah replied, "well, it's not very good news. The shoe prints that they photographed match the database, but they are from the most popular male shoe of the season—thousands sold on a single day. And the tire pattern is also in the database. But it's a tire that ships on all Toyota Camrys. So it could basically match any Camry with original tires that was purchased in the last four years."

"That's nothing to go on," said Mark. "They also didn't find any fingerprints, and they don't have a camera system."

"At least we know from the shoes that it's a male—and most likely a male in his teens or twenties with a taste for expensive athletic shoes. Probably lower-income—that's the typical profile of the guys who wait in line for hours to buy these things."

"Lower-income but still has the money to buy expensive shoes?" Mark asked.

"That's the world we live in. Shoes before food with these guys."

"Isn't that classist, Shaynah?"

"Not if it's true. Most expensive athletic shoes are purchased by lower-income men. But we're never going to be able to catch him by tracking him down by the footprints, at least not until he hits something with better security. We need a camera image—or at least a nearby gas station with a camera."

"I agree," said Mark. "And unfortunately, I think he knows that. He's only hit small niche museums with little security in the middle of nowhere."

"I've been trying to see if anyone is selling either the quilt or the airplane, but nothing has come up," said Shaynah.

"I did the whole pawn shop routine, and nothing there either."

"Do you think we should warn some of the smaller museums in Minnesota that have stuff from famous people?" Shaynah asked.

"Yeah, I was thinking that too. I'll talk to Hill about it. What other targets do you think he'll strike? Paisley Park in Chanhassen?"

"Maybe. Have you been there? I wonder what the security is like," Shaynah said.

"I didn't care for the man or his music, so I wouldn't want to go there for a visit. But we can find out what they have going on for security. They could be a big target."

"I'm sure you know that Judy Garland is from Grand Rapids," Shaynah said. "I think they have a pair of actual ruby slippers that were used in *The Wizard of Oz*. We might want to keep an eye on those."

"Now," Mark replied, "why would I know anything about Judy Garland? Are you making another assumption?"

"That you're a friend of Dorothy? Yep, I am."

"Fair enough. We should find out if Hibbing or Duluth has any Robert Zimmerman crap lying around."

"Who's that?" Shaynah asked.

"Bob Dylan."

"Really? Didn't know what his birth name was but knew he was from somewhere up there. Any sports stars from this state?"

"Ha! First you say I'm a friend of Dorothy, but now you assume I know about sports. Make up your mind."

"Well, do you know anything about famous Minnesotan sports stars?" Shaynah asked.

"No."

"Well, there you go."

"I'll try to find some online. Let's each make a list of things we think might be at risk and get together tomorrow."

"Fine. But you stick to the show people and leave the sports to me."

The drive from Little Falls back to St. Paul was just ten minutes short of two hours. Mark drove while Shaynah worked on her laptop, researching famous Minnesotans and their museums. They were on Minnesota Highway 10, having just passed the exit for the town of Sartell, when Shaynah's phone rang.

She looked at the screen and answered it. "What do you … okay … ah, probably. Well, of course I'm not happy about it, but I'm not going to keep you on a lease if you're moving out. I wish you'd just … no … I know, but … okay. Whatever. I can afford the apartment on my own. Don't worry, I'll take you off the lease. I'll send you a new copy. Bye."

They sat in silence for about a mile before Mark sighed and asked, "What was that all about?"

"Ugh. My fiancé is moving out. Well, I guess I need to get used to not calling him my fiancé. So this guy that I was previously going to marry is moving out and moving on."

"I'm sorry to hear that—I really am. That's rough. Why?"

"He thinks that we're too young, and he's not ready to settle down yet. You know, it's the typical male shit. He wants to see other people and live a little and then decide if we're right for each other. So that's that. Straight guys are all like that."

"Well," Mark replied, "he sounds smart to me."

"What?" Shaynah yelled. "Now I know that we don't always get along, but Christ, Mark, what a terrible thing to say! He's smart for leaving me. Thanks a lot for the support."

"No, seriously, he is. Listen, Shaynah, this has a lot less to do with you than you think. You are too young to get married. You're just a year out of college. Is he the same age?"

"Yes," Shaynah said reluctantly.

"Well, there you go. The two of you are way too young. Both of you will regret it if you get married now. You need to see what's out there and live a little. When you're in your thirties, then you'll know. He's actually doing you a huge favor, and you should thank him. Do you want to be married to a man that wakes up at thirty-five, looks at you sleeping next to him and the baby between you, and shows deep resentment? No, you don't."

"But that's not what it would be like. If you love someone, it's forever. Even if you get tired of it."

"Well," said Mark, "you don't understand love. Love gets way more attention than it deserves. Now the emotion of 'like'—that's the emotion we should sing songs about. Liking someone is much more important that loving someone. You just think about that."

"What's your—I know you hate 'husband'—partner? What's his name?"

"Andrew. But we hate 'partner' too. He's my friend."

"What the hell, Mark?" Shaynah replied. "Now I am going to really get on your case. Millions of people fought hard so that same-sex couples could marry, and now you go and call each other friends? That's ridiculous. What? He's your friend that you live with and sleep with every night and share your life with? How can you be okay with that?"

"I'm not from your generation. To us, 'friend' is the best word that describes what we are. Yep, we do live together, own a house together, and sleep together. But we've been friends for a long time, and that's probably not going to change."

"Well, do you love him? I mean, do you like him?"

"I like being with him. I can't imagine not seeing him every day.

But we were in our thirties when we met. You can't like someone if you don't even know what you like yourself. Trust me, Shaynah. Let the guy move out—you're doing the right thing by letting him off the lease without a fight. Move on. Date a lot of guys. And one day, you'll be so glad that you let this guy find out what he likes too. Anyway, that's enough talk of that. How's your list going?"

"Besides Judy Garland, I've got Mary Tyler Moore, Charles Schulz, the Mayo brothers, the Coen brothers, and Jessica Lange."

"Mary Tyler Moore never lived in Minneapolis. Just her character Mary Richards did. And don't forget about Jesse Ventura."

"Okay. I'll delete Mary Tyler Moore and add Ventura. But I think the only people on this list that have a museum are the Mayo brothers—there's a museum at the Mayo Clinic down in Rochester. I've never been there."

"I haven't either," said Mark. "But we should give them a call and see what kind of security they have around there."

10

EZEKIEL SLEEPS

"Ezekiel Smith," said the young man's father, "you may say the blessing tonight."

Mrs. Smith and the other six Smith children looked at Ezekiel with amazement.

"Wow, Zeke," said one of the little Smiths excitedly, "you must be all grown up now!"

"His name is Ezekiel," the father replied, "and yes, he is old enough now that he can say the blessing. But we still need to hold hands and be as respectful as if I was saying it."

Mrs. Smith gave Ezekiel a big smile and reached her hands to the children on either side of her.

Ezekiel cleared his throat. "Heavenly Father," he began, "we thank you for this food we are about to eat. And we thank you for each other. Please keep us safe and healthy. Amen."

The other Smiths were just starting to repeat the "Amen" when Mr. Smith interrupted. "You forgot to offer praise."

"Oh yes," said Ezekiel. "Sorry about that. Heavenly Father, we thank you for this food we are about to eat. We praise your holy name because you are the source of all life. We will be obedient to you now and always. And we thank you for each other. Please keep us safe and healthy. Amen."

"Amen," said all those around the table in unison.

"That was a fine prayer," said Mrs. Smith. "Maybe someday you'll be the leader of a whole church, just like your father."

"Well," Mr. Smith replied, "he'll have a long way to go. But if he works hard, he may get there. And I don't mean working hard at that restaurant where you're working now, Ezekiel. That's fine for now—and it's probably good to have experience working with heathens. But soon you'll need a good Christian job. Geno's can teach you responsibility, but not how to act in the place of Jesus Christ, our Lord and savior."

"Yes, Daddy," Ezekiel replied.

They ate the rest of their dinner while listening to Mr. Smith talk about his sermon for that Sunday's service at the Lake Superior Celebration Church. Mrs. Smith agreed with everything her husband said.

After dinner, Ezekiel went to his room and closed the door. There, he became Zeke. He hated his name—like he hated most of his life. He had just turned eighteen and was about to graduate from a Christian high school. He wanted nothing more than to take the money he'd earned at Geno's Restaurant and move to Minneapolis to attend the University of Minnesota.

For the last year, he'd told his parents that he was planning on attending Crossroads Bible College in Rochester, Minnesota. Even though he'd applied there and been accepted—and had his parents pay the housing fee—he had no intention of ever going to that college. His plan was to cut all ties with them and become an independent student. He knew it wouldn't be easy and would take an extra year of working in Minneapolis before he could be a student. But it would be worth it.

Whereas Ezekiel Smith was a pious, perfect boy, Zeke Smith was gay. However, he was not one of those gay teenagers who moped around, and he wasn't one of those activist types either. He'd always known he was gay and didn't have a problem with it. He didn't care what his parents or their church thought.

Zeke was tall and blond. He'd been active on the swimming team at his high school and had the body to prove it. He often wondered if he could have been a competitive swimmer along with the public-school kids. But since his Christian school did not participate in organized sports with regular schools, he had no way of knowing how good he really was.

His biggest issue was that he was an eighteen-year-old virgin who each night felt the pangs of being human. Simply put, he wanted to have sex. He wanted to have sex with a man. And he couldn't wait much longer. He had been taught to meditate on the name Jesus before going to bed in order to calm down. But most nights, Zeke meditated on the name Minneapolis.

When that didn't work, and he wasn't able to control his humanity, he thought about the manager of the restaurant. He was older but had a great body. Zeke was infatuated with Craig Kellerman and often thought about him as he cuddled his pillow at night.

11

THE THREE PRESIDENTS

M arge had just finished a piece of coffee cake and a mug of coffee in her kitchen in Walnut Grove, Minnesota, when the kitchen phone rang. Even though she had a cell phone, only her grandkids ever called her on that. She got up from her table covered in a plastic Easter tablecloth and answered the clanging phone that was attached to the wall.

"Hello?"

"Hello, is this the Gundersons of Walnut Grove?" said an older female voice on the phone.

"I'm looking for Margie Gunderson."

"Yes, this is Marge Gunderson—I go by Marge, not Margie."

"Oh dear, I'll remember. Say, my name is Frances Schultz, and I'm the president of the Sinclair Lewis Society up here in Sauk Centre. Do you know of Sinclair Lewis?"

"The author?"

"Yes, of course. And Marge, are you still the president of the Laura Ingalls Wilder Auxiliary?"

"Yes, I am," Marge replied.

"Oh, good. Well, I'm calling because—say, did you know that Sinclair Lewis and Laura Ingalls Wilder knew each other?"

"No, I don't believe that I did know that."

"Well, Sinclair's second wife, Dorothy Thompson, was a really good friend of Rose Wilder. That would be Laura's—"

"Laura's daughter, yes, I know who she is."

"Oh, of course you would."

"Is that why you're calling?" Marge asked.

"No, I wish it was, but this is sadder and more important. I heard from some investigators that someone took Laura Wilder's quilt just recently. Is that right?"

"Yes, it's very sad for us."

"I'll bet is it. But see, we had something taken from us just two nights ago too. The urn that held Sinclair Lewis's ashes when they were sent from Europe was stolen from our museum. It's just terrible. I feel like a piece of Sinclair is gone forever."

"That is terrible," said Marge. "Is this related to what happened here in Walnut Grove?"

"Well, I think so. See, the people that investigate these things in St. Paul didn't want us knowing all this. But my son-in-law is the chief of police in Sauk Centre, and he told me that they told him about Laura's quilt and one more thing—someone also broke into the Charles Lindbergh museum in Little Falls and ran off with his first toy airplane."

"That's just awful. My goodness, this is terrible," said Marge. "What kind of a world is this?"

"That's what I said to my son-in-law. So my daughter is a huge fan of Sinclair's, just like her parents, and she's really upset. So my son-in-law wasn't supposed to tell me this, but he did because he's upset with the people in St. Paul. They told him that they want to keep this all quiet and just focus on getting better security for the small museums. But my son-in-law, the chief of police, and I think that we need to take this to another level."

"What do you have in mind?"

"Well, I called over to Little Falls and talked to their president, a nice man named Hank. We think that we should go public with this—you know, talk to the papers. If we get some pictures of the missing items out there, maybe someone can locate them."

"You know, that might not be a bad idea. I really don't care if they actually catch anyone, but I sure would like Laura's quilt back."

"Well, I do care that they catch someone. But yes, I agree that I'd want the urn back first and then see these people face a judge second. Say, do you think you can come up to Willmar sometime? Hank said he'd pick me up, and Willmar is about halfway between Walnut Grove and Sauk Centre."

"I'll have to check with my daughter. My husband has passed on, and he did all the driving out of town. I can drive anyway in Walnut Grove, of course, but not on the highway."

"Oh, that's no problem. I'll give you my number, and maybe we can meet this Saturday."

12

A SALSA WITH SINCLAIR LEWIS

Craig got home late from the restaurant. He was tired and hungry. On his way out, he had grabbed a vacuum-sealed bag of salsa and a bag of tortilla chips. *I shouldn't eat this crap. But I'm starving, and there's nothing else around. I'll have to run an extra three tomorrow.* Now he plopped himself on his couch and turned on *Forensic Files.* He tore open the bag of salsa on the perforated lines and dumped the entire contents into the Sinclair Lewis cremation urn. *I might try to keep this thing. It's useful. I wonder if that puts me in any danger. I'll think about it.*

It was late April but still cold outside. Small flecks of frozen rain clinked against his windows. *I should have moved away from this lousy Duluth weather as soon as I was done with college. Now I'm stuck here.*

He opened the bag of chips and started dipping them into the urn. *I probably should have washed this thing first. Oh well, nobody has touched it in years, and a little Sinclair Lewis DNA can't hurt. I mean, the guy was absolutely brilliant.*

He ate for a few minutes and then lost interest in the television show. He began to study the urn to see if it had any markings that could be traced. *This is not at all like the urn where my mom's ashes were kept. But you couldn't really even call that one an urn; it was more of a cardboard box.*

I remember Dad yelling at me to get dressed. I must have been about seven. He said that my aunt was going to pick me up. I hadn't even known I had an aunt. He said that my mom had died and that my aunt wanted to take me to the funeral so that the family wouldn't talk about my not being there. I asked, What happened to her? He told me that she stuck a gun in her mouth and blew out her brains. He said that the brains had landed all over the room and ruined the carpet. Then he said that she'd done it because she knew that her son Craig was a retard, and she hated him. That's how he told me that my mom had died.

My aunt was mean. She said I looked like my dad. I don't remember her name. But she made me stand next to the cardboard box of ashes and look sad. I had to stand there a long time. She'd poke me to look sadder when certain people passed by. She must have been wanting sympathy money. I never saw a dime of that. I wonder where my mom actually blew her brains out. I guess I wouldn't be able to find out now—I have no idea if I have any relatives left up there. Probably not. Hopefully not. They probably all died of alcohol and diabetes.

He dipped some more chips into the salsa, then abruptly set the whole urn on his coffee table. *I've eaten enough. I need to go for a run. It'll be cold. I better put on my winter running gear. I need to get in shape for the next one. It's big. That goddamn stupid Kensington Runestone. What a dumb-ass piece of shit that thing is.*

13

READ ALL ABOUT IT

"Hey, Shaynah, have you seen this?" Mark asked as he stormed into Shaynah's office early in the morning. He was waving a copy of the Minneapolis *Star Tribune* newspaper.

"What's that? A newspaper?" she replied. "Yeah, I saw one once in a museum."

"No, it's not funny. It's about us."

"What?"

He turned the paper around and pointed to a headline on the front page. It wasn't the top story, but the headline was still large enough to garner attention: "Rash of Historical Thefts Leaves Museums in a Panic."

"How did that get out?" Shaynah asked. "And what kind of headline is that—overreact much?"

"It looks like some of the leaders of the museums got together and contacted the Strib. I'm not sure how they all found out about each other's thefts. But I guess these museum folks are a tight knit group. We should have anticipated that they would find out and take action on their own. We dropped the ball on this one, probably."

"What does it say?" Shaynah asked.

"Not much, really. Just that Walnut Grove, Little Falls, and Sauk Centre were all hit. They got all the items correct, but there isn't much else to report because, well, there isn't much else that we even know."

"Have you seen the director about it yet?"

"Yeah, Hill stopped me on my way to see you—thinks it's a good thing and probably the end of the story. Other museums in the state will probably beef up security, and the press might scare away whoever has been doing it."

"But it does mean that we'll most likely never see the items again."

"Yep. Marge Gunderson is quoted in the article. I'm sure she has no idea that she just as good as burned that quilt herself," said Mark.

"Do you think Hill is right? That this will be the end of it? That the publicity will make it too hard for the thief to continue?"

"I'm not so sure. Yeah, I think the word will spread around to small county museums, and they'll get some cameras. But as far as the perp goes, it could go two ways. He may feel satisfied that he made the news and stop. Or he might want more attention and decide to raise the ante."

"I was thinking that same thing. But listen, I was thinking last night—now that I live alone, I have a lot more time to myself—we know that the shoes from the footprints in Little Falls had to have been purchased in the spring because that's when they came out. We can also make a fairly good assumption that the thief is from Minnesota due to the nature of the crimes. Now most of the young guys who bought those shoes—if not all of them—would have paid for them with a credit card. But I'm willing to bet that our guy used cash. How hard would it be to locate all the stores that sold those shoes, find out which had cash transactions, and then use the store cameras to get a look?"

"Shoot, Shaynah," Mark replied. "That's an awful lot of work. But I guess it could be done. You want to start by getting a list of stores that sold that exact shoe?"

"I've already started it."

"I'm sure that whoever it is has already either destroyed or sold off the quilt and the toy plane—they've had plenty of time to do that. But we might be able to save Sinclair's urn. That one would be harder to hide or destroy."

14

LOEB FINDS LEOPOLD

Well, I guess it's hit the news, and my fun time is over. Craig sat at his desk inside the manager's office at the restaurant. On the desk sat a copy of the *Duluth News Tribune*. They had run the same story as reported by the Minneapolis paper, except the thefts were the main headline because nothing else had occurred in Duluth the day prior.

Craig was exhilarated and depressed at the same time. *I made it into the news! And not only that, but it says that investigators are baffled and have no clues. I really did it. But now I'm probably done. Any other museum with stuff from a famous person is going to be on alert. Depressing.*

He drank from a glass of Diet Coke that he'd grabbed from the fountain machine in the beverage station—one of the perks of his job. It was his turn to take the evening shift, and since it was still afternoon, he needed the caffeine. *I wonder if I should get rid of the Lewis urn. But how would I go about doing that? Maybe I'll just hide it somewhere—that way there will always be something that's just mine even though other people want it.*

There was a knock at the door.

"Come in," Craig said.

The door opened, and Zeke walked through, carrying his backpack.

"Are you busy?" Zeke asked. "Or can I do some homework in here until my shift starts?"

"No problem," Craig answered. "Make yourself at home."

Zeke placed his backpack on a side table, grabbed a chair from near Craig's desk, and sat down. He opened the backpack and took out his laptop.

Poor kid. Doesn't have many friends, if he even has one. Prefers to do his homework in here instead of with the others in the break room. Goddamn religion has him brainwashed. He's probably gay—he seems very gay. I think he has a crush on me. "Are you still going ahead with your plan to move to Minneapolis after graduation?" Craig asked.

Zeke turned around in his chair and caught the door with his foot. He slowly closed it.

Shoot. He must want to keep it a secret. "Sorry," said Craig, "I forgot that you haven't told anyone else."

"No worry," said Zeke. "I just don't want my parents finding out because they'll find a way to stop it. You're the only person I've told."

That's actually kind of sweet. It makes me feel good. "So how does this whole thing work? Will you live off minimum wage?"

"Yeah, it's going to be hard. But I only have to do it for one year. See, in Minnesota, I have to live on my own for a year and not take any college courses. Then I can apply to become an independent student. Because I'll have no money, I can get a lot of financial aid. That should help."

"Can you live down there on minimum wage? Do you have an apartment?"

"I've got a few leads. But it's been rough because it's not like I can ask my parents to help me or anything."

"Are you the oldest?"

"Yep."

Poor kid.

Craig went back to working on the restaurant's schedule, and Zeke started his homework.

He is a poor kid in the financial sense too. But I was a really poor kid once, and I was able to go to college and do okay. But of course, I had no parents by that time, and this kid has to spend a year making it so that he has no parents. I should stay in contact with him. It might be fun to watch someone else struggle for once.

I'm going to do the runestone. It doesn't belong to anyone famous, and maybe the museum won't have time to get extra security. But the damn thing weighs 202 pounds. I need to find a way to deal with that. It will be my big finale. So the runestone will be the end of all of this. Depressing.

Christ! Why do I get excited when I think about this kid failing? I'd really like to see him fail—just so that his stupid religious dad can feel it. I'd love to see his dad's pious face when he finds out that his gay son is living with another man. What if that son was caught stealing something? Pastor Dad would be humiliated in front of his church. I'd love to see that. Maybe ...

"Hey, Zeke," said Craig, "I've got an idea. I live in a house on the hillside. It's got too much room for one person, and I was thinking about getting a roommate—not so much for the money, but just to have someone around once in a while. If you're interested, and if you think you can put Minneapolis on hold for a year, you're welcome to move in with me. You can keep your job at the restaurant. You don't have to pay me anything—just keep the house clean, mow the lawn, do the snow, that kind of stuff. You could put all your money away—or better yet, give all your money to me as rent, and I'll put it in an account and give it back to you. That way, you wouldn't have to declare it and lower your financial aid."

"Really? That's ... I don't know. Are you sure?"

"Sure. It will give me a chance to decide if I really do like living with someone else. Sort of like a dry run on having a roommate. You're a good kid, and I'd like to help out. You know, I've told you a little about me, but I'm not sure if I told you that I started with nothing. I didn't have any real parents. I'd sort of like to do this for you—to give back, I guess."

"It might be hard being in Duluth and this close to my parents," Zeke said.

"You're eighteen. There's not a damn thing they can do about it."

"In my parents' house, 'damn' is a swear word."

"That's why you really need to come live with me. I can teach you words that are way worse than 'damn.'"

15

THE SMALL VIKING SHIP

The Kensington Runestone had been discovered by Olof Ohman in 1898 near the small town of Kensington, Minnesota. It was a big rock with runes of a Scandinavian language carved on it. The writing told of a group of Norwegians who had passed through what was now Minnesota in the year 1362.

Some thought it proved that the Vikings had arrived in North America before Columbus and that the first contact between Europe and the United States had occurred in Minnesota. In the town of Alexandria, Minnesota, right along Lake Agnes, was the Runestone Museum. A large statue of a Viking stood nearby. His shield bore the inscription "Alexandria, Birthplace of America."

Not one scholar had been able to verify the runestone. The linguistics of the text matched nineteenth-century Swedish more than fourteenth-century Norwegian. The actual rune carvings were too sharply cut to have been lying out in the weather for over five hundred years. Most likely, the whole thing was a hoax conceived by Olof Ohman. Still, many people in the local area swore that it was the real deal.

Craig Kellerman, under an assumed name, rented a cabin on

Lake Agnes for the weekend. It was still a bit cold out, but all the ice on the lake had disappeared. When he arrived in his rental vehicle, he opened the driver's door, set a wheelchair—also rented—outside the door, and swung his body down into the chair. He'd practiced with the chair a lot since stealing the urn.

The cabin came with a pontoon. Craig assumed that the owner of the cabin would be apprehensive about a disabled person using a pontoon. He did all he could to show the woman that he was quite capable. He was there to relax on the lake before the fishing season started—that was his official statement.

Late on Saturday afternoon, Craig wheeled himself onto the pontoon and started the motor. He floated around for a bit, practicing how to drive quietly, and then let it float about. The sky grew dark. He laid on the cushioned bench of the pontoon and breathed. *I can afford to rent a cabin and be out on the lake in a private pontoon. I'm not scared of the water.* His mind wandered back to a time in elementary school when some other boys were forcing his head into a toilet. *I couldn't breathe. I thought I was going to die. They kept yelling about how my dad was a druggie and my mom was crazy and I was their retarded kid. They called me a faggot. Why do bullies always call me a faggot? I'm not gay. Maybe that's the only word they know.*

At some point he fell asleep. When he woke, it was completely dark all around the lake. He could see lights on the shore, but nothing reflected off the still water around him. He got up, took off his clothes, and dressed all in black. He put on his gloves and another pair of new tennis shoes. He checked his watch—2:47 a.m. *Just about right. Now start the trolling motor, slow and quiet.*

It took a while for the pontoon to reach the far end of Lake Agnes, whose shore was next to the city of Alexandria. He'd located a city dock a week ago. The dock closed at sundown. The city had an ordinance against boaters being loud at night. There was no need for lights on the dock, and nobody was around.

Craig stopped the motor, jumped onto the dock, and quietly tied up the pontoon. Then he grabbed the wheelchair and ran swiftly toward the museum with the chair on his back. It was only a few hundred feet through the darkness. *They might have an alarm, but not cameras—or at least there weren't any the last time I was here. Work fast. Just get it done.*

He ran through a few trees that lined the back of the property. Everything was very quiet in town. He saw the back door, ran toward it, and set the wheelchair on the ground next to it. He tried his universal lock pick on the back door. *Christ! It worked! That saves me a lot of time.*

Grabbing the wheelchair, he opened the door and stepped inside. The space was small. No alarm sounded. *Might be a silent alarm. And the police station is very close. Hurry.*

The Kensington Runestone sat atop a wooden platform in the middle of the museum. It was thirty inches long from top to bottom. Four pieces of plexiglass surrounded the stone, but the top was completely open. Craig grabbed the top of one of the sides and pulled. It gave a little. He then hung from the plexiglass with all his weight, and the entire side split from the others and fell to the floor. He immediately ran and removed the opposite side of plexiglass in the same way.

Now I'll see if this will work. If not, just get the hell out of here and leave the goddamn stone for someone else to deal with. Craig pushed the wheelchair right up to the wooden platform and set both brakes on the chair. Then he walked around to the other side and pushed on the stone. The runestone was six inches thick, and because it was a bit top-heavy, it easily started to wobble. He gave it one great push, and it fell completely over and off the side of the platform. There was a sound as it fell, but it wasn't too loud. Craig ran around to the other side.

The runestone had hit the wheelchair, but only half of it was against the seat. The other side of the stone was resting against the platform. The vinyl seat of the wheelchair was starting to tear. Craig had a tremendous amount of adrenaline. Since half the weight of the stone was already on the wheelchair, he just needed to push on the other half. He grunted and used his back. Looking at the result, he thought, *Wow, I can't believe I just did that.* Some of the stone was hanging off the edge of the chair, but he'd known it would be too big. *Let's just hope I can push it before it tears through the seat. But these chairs must hold more than two hundred pounds. Maybe I should have gotten the bigger wheelchair? But then I would have looked stupid in it when I got to the resort cabin. I hope they don't notice tomorrow that I'm a disabled person in a ripped wheelchair.*

Craig pushed the stone through the museum and out the back door, onto the wet grass. He didn't take time to close the door. *I wish I could have looked around and soaked it all in. I always enjoy that part—the danger of being caught. But not this time.*

Surprisingly, the wheelchair pushed easily over the grass. The weight of the stone gave the chair sustenance and momentum. He continued without stopping, and the momentum was so great that he easily pushed the chair onto the dock and onto the pontoon. Everything came to a stop with a massive crash when the wheelchair carrying the stone finally hit the pontoon's railing. Craig looked around. *Still no one in sight. It's a good thing it didn't break the railing—that woman at the resort seemed like she would be mad at that sort of thing.*

He untied the pontoon, started the motor, and trolled out over the black water. And there, in the middle of Lake Agnes, he did what he had always planned to do. *Nobody else will ever have this stone—real or not. It will always be mine. I will never tell anyone else what I did with it. When I die, knowledge of this stone's location will die.*

He opened the side gate of the pontoon, pushed the runestone over to it, and then shoved it completely overboard. In less than a second, it was gone. *Elaborate hoax or proof of Viking explorers? Only the fish of Lake Agnes can investigate now.*

16

STONE-COLD RUNE

It had been a long day for Mark. After a morning of bouncing around ideas with Director Hill of the BCA, he and Shaynah had driven to Alexandria to start the investigation of the missing Kensington Runestone. The museum had a silent alarm, and they knew what time the theft had occurred. But as with the crimes in Walnut Grove, Little Falls, and Sauk Centre, that was about all they knew.

Mark stood in the cool spring air and stared at the large statue of a Viking. He had relatives in the area, whom he had not spoken with in three decades, and knew that they referred to the statue as "Big Ole." Mark hated that name. One of his passions was studying the history of World's Fairs. He knew that the statue had been created for the Minnesota Pavilion at the 1964–65 World's Fair in New York City. He also knew that the runestone had been displayed at that fair. He sighed deeply, knowing that he was under immense pressure to return to St. Paul with at least one significant lead.

He saw Shaynah exit the liquor store next door to the Runestone Museum and head toward him. She looked disappointed. Her look made his heart feel even heavier than it already was.

"No luck?" Mark asked.

"Oh, there's footage all right," she replied. "They have a camera, and it recorded the whole street for the whole night. But there's nothing on the video—no cars around when the alarm sounded until the local cops showed up. It had to have been taken through the back door."

"Then there has to be more than one of them. No one person could carry a 202-pound stone."

"But where did they go? Even two people couldn't have carried it far. There are no streets back there."

"Let's go back and look again. We just can't go home without something to report—even if it's just some broken twigs."

They walked around the side of the museum. The backyard of the main structure contained several small recreations of historic buildings. This was a place for school kids to explore on their field trips after they had finished looking at the runestone.

"This is one time I wish the winter had lasted longer," said Shaynah. "It would be better if they'd had some snow to leave tracks in. This is all grass up to the bike trail and then the lake."

"You know," said Mark, "the lake could be where they went. Maybe they had a getaway boat instead of a getaway car."

"That's a pretty good idea, but we need something more to back it up. Come over here and look at this."

Mark followed her over to a shallow spot in the grass. Water had collected in a shallow depression, and the grass under it was matted down. "What do you see?" Mark asked.

"Right there. Do you see those two lines in the grass under the water? You can barely make them out."

Mark bent down to get a good look. "Yep. And they are perfectly straight. Lawn mower?"

"It's too early in the year for lawn mowers, and there aren't any other lawn mower marks anywhere else. Do you have a tape measure?"

"Of course."

"I knew you would."

Mark reached into his pants pocket and pulled out a small plastic cylinder that contained a tiny retractable tape measure. "What do you want to know?" he asked. "Length? Width?"

"The width between the two lines."

Mark bent down, measured, and said, "Twenty-six inches. Too wide for a lawn mower."

"But exactly the measurement of space between two wheels of a standard wheelchair. It was one person. He somehow got the rune-stone onto a wheelchair and pushed it across the grass, over the bike trail, and right out onto the dock. Easy. I guess it also could have been some sort of cart with the same wheel width, but it's the same concept anyway."

Mark, without saying anything, walked in a straight line from the wet grass to the dock on Lake Agnes. Shaynah followed, a few paces behind.

"Here," Mark said, pointing to a place between the historical buildings. "In this mud there are the same wheels marks, plus foot tracks—one set of foot tracks. And over here by the bike trail—more of the same."

Shaynah took her good camera out of her purse and started to photograph what they had found. "What do you do with a 202-pound stone with weird carvings on it anyway?" she asked as she worked.

"Well, unlike the other things he took, this is pretty much impossible to destroy. I doubt it's worth anything on the black market since it didn't belong to anyone famous and is probably a fake anyway."

"Shh, don't say that so loud. That old guy in the museum it terribly distraught over it. He says it's absolutely real proof that the Vikings were here before Columbus."

"Yeah, well, why didn't they spend a few dollars on a security camera then?"

17

ZEKE AWAKENS

Spring finally came to Duluth, Minnesota, just in time for graduation season. Craig usually hated this time of year because it was a scheduling nightmare at the restaurant—everyone wanted off to attend parties and associated events. But this year, he was looking forward to welcoming Zeke into his home. He genuinely wanted the company. *Now that I've taken a break from museum theft, I need another focus. I want an accomplice that's all mine. I want his dad to feel the pain of having a bad son. Zeke can be a bad son—I know he can.*

Christ! I never got around to hiding that damn urn under the ground somewhere. I'll just throw it under the kitchen sink. Good enough. And I'll keep the supply cabinet downstairs locked, at least until I'm ready to spring it on him. He's going to need a lot of training.

On the day after Zeke's graduation, Craig's doorbell rang. Craig answered the door and saw that Zeke was wearing a backpack and carrying two large suitcases.

"Is that all your stuff?" Craig asked.

"It's all I could carry on the bus," Zeke replied.

"You took the bus?"

"Yep. I'm not going to be able to use my car since my parents own it. But I've saved enough from working to buy a junker."

"We'll take care of that this week. Come on in."

Craig gave him a tour of the small house. He showed Zeke the second bedroom and instructed him to put all his stuff in there.

"So it didn't go so well with your parents, I take it," Craig said.

"It was what I had expected. I let them have yesterday. But I took today. I told them this morning that I was leaving. They think I'm in Minneapolis. I'm sad for the other kids in the house, but I have to think of me now."

"I think that's very wise. You can't help others until you help yourself. We'll get you a car, and then you can be on your way to starting a new life. Also, I'm going to recommend that you get a raise at work since it will be your full-time career for the next year."

"Wow, Craig. I mean, I don't how to thank you for all this. I'm so grate—"

Craig stopped listening, lost in his own thoughts. *It's been a rough couple of days for him. But he'll have rougher days ahead. The guy has got to be gay—I'm counting on it. I wonder what it will be like. I've slept with several women before, but not for a while. I wonder if I can do it with a guy. I guess I just need to focus like the therapist said. At least he's young and clean—that helps. And he's got a huge crush on me—that helps too. I just need to make him want it. That should be easy too. I'm in pretty good shape.*

"I really do," Zeke continued. "Seriously, I will pay you back someday."

"I'm sure you will," Craig replied. "But you don't need to worry about that now. Anyway, let me show you the bathroom. This is a one-bathroom house, so we'll have to share. I hope you won't mind if you catch me coming out of the shower with just a towel on. I promise that I won't mind if I happen to catch you."

Craig turned in the small hallway and winked at Zeke. He saw Zeke smile a little. *The seed is planted. Now let's see what happens.*

Zeke couldn't believe what he'd just heard as he followed Craig into the bathroom. *I'm so happy right now. He winked at me. Oh God, I hope I see him coming out of the shower wearing a towel. I hope he likes me. When he winked, my stomach felt excited, and it's hard to breathe right now. I really hope I don't ever make him mad at me. I want to stay living here for a long time.*

18

A FAMILY AFFAIR

As the weeks went on, life at the Kellerman/Smith household settled into a routine, with the roommates working at the restaurant, watching television late into the night, and sleeping in through the morning. Zeke was elated with his new life. He hadn't heard a word from his family and had no idea whether they knew he was still in Duluth or not.

Craig took Zeke to a used-car dealer that he'd known for a few years. They purchased a four-year-old Nissan Versa with 58,000 miles on it. It cost more than Zeke wanted to pay, but Craig made up the difference. He told Zeke that he planned on using it from time to time.

Zeke liked that Craig continued to drop intimate hints. He loved the moments when Craig would brush against him in the kitchen or join him while he was brushing his teeth. Zeke didn't want to seem like he was intruding on Craig's privacy, but it was difficult when Craig always seemed to be wearing a towel in the bathroom and cleaning the living room shirtless. Zeke had also started to join Craig on his long runs around Duluth.

Because he wanted to make and save as much money as possible, Zeke took every extra shift at the restaurant. Unexpectedly, time at work moved faster than it had before he'd moved in with Craig.

Having something to look forward to at the end of the day made everything better. Zeke especially liked it when he worked later than Craig. He liked the idea of driving home to Craig, who was already on the couch, watching true-crime television in his pajamas.

By the end of June, Zeke had become quite accustomed to his new life. As he excitedly drove home after work one night, he thought, *I wonder if I should stop and buy flowers at the grocery store. Craig really liked them last week—he even put them in the weird brass vase from under the sink. God, I really want him to kiss me. Does he like me that way, or am I making too much of him? Maybe he's just friendly with everyone and wants me to feel like I'm at home. That's probably it. How do I know if he's gay?*

If I'd known this is what a family is supposed to feel like, I would have left home a long time ago. God, I wasted so much time living there. I wish that they'd be driving around sometime and see me and Craig out for a run—especially if we aren't wearing shirts. What would they say? Maybe I wouldn't want to know. But I probably do know.

I can't forget when I was fourteen and Mom told me that Dad wanted to see me at the church. I rode my bike there, and he was waiting for me. We sat in a pew, and he told me that Mom was afraid I was a homosexual, and he wanted to put a stop to that. I had to recite from Leviticus time and time again. And there was all that stupid crap about Sodom and Gomorrah, where God hates homosexuals but loves it when the daughters get their dad drunk and have sex with him.

He was on me all the damn time. "Don't sit like that—don't cross your legs like that; you look like a faggot. You have to be in swimming. Don't even think of trying out for that play. Your mom still thinks you're queer and wants to send you away to a camp. You better shape up, or we'll do just that."

God, I hated all that religious shit. It was all power in disguise. I want them to see us running without shirts—that would really show them. I'm going to stop and get flowers for Craig. I hope he's not just being nice. What if he doesn't really mean anything by hinting like he does so much? I want him to touch me so badly.

Zeke took a turn and drove past the iron fence that separated the Glensheen estate from the rest of the world. The enormous mansion rose up between the fence and Lake Superior. *There's Glensheen. That's where the murders happened.*

19

LOEB BEFORE LEOPOLD

After weeks of teasing, Craig was anxious for Zeke to get home from the restaurant's late shift. He'd decided that it was time to reel him in. *I finally get to see if I can pull it off. He just about busts every time he sees me cleaning in my jeans, so getting him interested will be easy. I just need to focus on my task and follow through as if it were regular sex with a woman.*

He heard Zeke's car pull into the driveway and park in front of the single-stall garage. Zeke entered through the kitchen door, put his keys in a small bowl on the counter next to the refrigerator, and waved the flowers at Craig.

"You don't have to do that," said Craig. "I mean, I like having flowers around, but you should save all your money for college."

"They don't cost that much," Zeke replied. "And I owe you way more than flowers."

"I told you not to worry about what you owe me. We'll figure that out later."

"Should I put them in this thing again? Maybe I should buy a vase that looks like a vase."

"I like that thing. It's a family heirloom."

Zeke grabbed the Sinclair Lewis urn from a countertop, filled it halfway with water, and stuck the flowers into it. He then took off his shoes and kicked them over by the door. Craig watched him enter the living room and sit in his usual chair.

"What are we watching?" Zeke asked. *"Forensic Files* again?"

"Yep," Craig answered. "It's an oldie but goodie." *Take it slow. Seem naive. Don't just make him want you; make him love you. Watch some episodes, get into talking about the crimes, then make your move. The goal is to have an accomplice and stick it to the dad—sex is a means to get there.*

After an hour of waiting and watching television, Craig said, "Hey, Zeke. Can I ask you something?"

"Sure, what?"

"I know you're from a religious family. And stop me if you don't want to talk about it—seriously, just stop me. But did you have a girlfriend or anything in high school?"

Zeke gave a small chuckle and said, "That's funny. I went to a Christian high school where my parents watched my every move. I didn't have a girlfriend."

"So you're a virgin?" *That got his attention—look at his eyes.* "Sorry, is that too much?"

"No, i-it's okay. Yeah, I'm a virgin, I guess."

"I know it's odd, but I'm a virgin too," said Craig.

"What? Seriously?"

"Yep. I might be the oldest one around. But I guess I wanted to wait for the right person—you know, someone that I feel comfortable around. I guess I got caught up with work and all that and never had the chance to meet the right person. Sorry if I'm getting too personal." *I know he's not sorry. Look at his expression. He wants this.*

"No, it's okay," Zeke replied. "I'm comfortable around here—oh, uh, not that I was—"

"Do you want to come and sit on the couch with me?" Craig asked.

Zeke didn't say anything but quickly got up from the chair and moved to the couch. He remained silent as they watched another six minutes of *Forensic Files.*

"Zeke," Craig said, "can I put my hand on your knee? Only if it's really okay—and I won't have any hard feelings if it's not. I mean, I'm gay, but I'm not sure if you are. So it's completely up to you. I want you to be comfortable, but I also want you to know that you are the person I'm comfortable around for the first time in my life." *He's completely going to fall for that.*

"Yeah, that would be okay—if you really want to."

Craig put his hand on Zeke's knee and looked into his eyes. *He has nice eyes—sort of like a woman's. I can work with that. Plus, the poor guy is eighteen and a virgin—it's not going to take that long.*

Craig leaned in and kissed Zeke hard on the lips. By the start of the next episode of *Forensic Files* they had moved to Craig's bedroom. By the second commercial break, Zeke was no longer a virgin.

One of Craig's best virtues was patience, at least when he wanted something bad enough. He had the patience to keep Zeke in his bed for a while. But he still wanted to get some sleep.

"This double bed isn't going to cut it," Craig said, holding Zeke's hand. "It's not enough room for me. If you're going to start sleeping in here, we need to get a queen- or king-size."

"Sounds good to me."

"The only thing is, I'm a little strapped for cash right now. Between your car and the extra utility expenses on the house, I don't have anything to spend on a bigger bed."

"I've got the money I've been saving."

"No. You need that for college. I would feel terrible taking it. Besides, if we're going to be in this together, then we need to start thinking about both our futures." *Keep using "we" and "us." He's falling for it.*

"I can pick up some more of Dylan's shifts. I think he wants to quit anyway."

"I've got a better idea. Do you guys still keep the cash tip money in a locker?"

"Yeah," Zeke replied hesitantly. "It's still the same as when I started."

"I've always thought that it was a bad system. But Karen's been the owner so long that she doesn't know how to do it better. Does she still run it to the bank when it's full?"

"Yeah, but not very often. Hardly anyone tips with cash anymore."

"How much do you think is in it now?"

"Probably a thousand or so. Whenever Karen decides to show up, she gets a server to let her into the locker. Then she takes it to the bank and divides it equally for our paychecks."

"See, that's a bad system. First of all, people tip for good service, but Karen divides it equally. It's not fair. Second, it's too easy to steal, even if only servers know the combination."

"Nobody would take it. That would be really bad for everyone. And it's just the cash tips—it's sort of fun to get as a bonus once in a while."

"You should take it," said Craig assertively. "The next time you work late, just take most of it—leave a hundred or so left."

"I'd never do that," Zeke replied.

"We could buy a bed. And you're a really good server. You deserve a much bigger cut. I'd do it myself, but the managers don't have access. Just take it."

20

FOLLOW THE MONEY

"Okay," said Mark, "I'm ready. What do you got?"

"All right," Shaynah replied. "Don't get your hopes up. But I'll have a report ready later this afternoon."

"By the way, Director Hill absolutely loves your reports. Not that I'm thrilled about it because it might mean more work for me—for all of us. But I thought you'd like to know."

"Thanks. And I'll help you. I seriously can't get enough of it. But anyway, I started by calling all the resorts located on Lake Agnes in Alexandria. It's not a huge lake by Minnesota standards, so it wasn't that difficult. Only one resort reported a guest that had a wheelchair, and he not only had one but was using it—like he was disabled."

"Really?" Mark replied. "That surprises me. I assumed he would have just taken the chair along. I guess he likes having a bit of a disguise."

"Oh, he does. So he made the reservation online and prepaid with a credit card. We tracked down the credit card. It belongs to a man in Duluth. However, he has a rock-solid alibi and can prove that his credit card number was taken because of several incorrect charges. Also, he's seventy-eight years old and doesn't match the description of the guy at the resort in the wheelchair."

"What's the description?"

"Well, the guy showed up and checked in, nothing unusual. He got a cabin right on the water. Then the resort owner trained him on how to use a pontoon. She spent enough time to get a good description. She thought he was in his mid-thirties, although he could have been older by the way he talked. She said he was in great shape—very athletic, very handsome. Dark perfectly trimmed beard. White guy. He was seated in the chair the whole time, so there is no height estimate. But his body shape is athletic, and he has dark hair. He was cleanly dressed and seemed altogether a well-put-together man. I mean, she seemed to be quite taken with him—almost infatuated."

"That can be a real problem. But how about a car? How'd he get there?"

"Yeah, she gave a description of a car. I got footage from several gas stations and other businesses in town. I've seen the car arriving and leaving the town from several locations. I was able to get a license plate from a camera at a bar. However, the plates were reported stolen from a church in Cloquet, up by Duluth. The church doesn't have cameras, so that's a dead end. But we might be able to limit our search to someone who lives in Duluth or the Iron Range. Since the identity theft occurred there, and the plates were taken there, it's a good place to start."

"When you were looking at the camera footage, did you see the runestone in the car when it was leaving town?"

"Nope, and I did look for it. But the stone would easily fit in the trunk, and there's no way he's going to drive around Alexandria, Minnesota, with the Kensington Runestone in his back seat."

"Yep, that's for sure. But I'm not sure that one guy could get the stone from a wheelchair into his trunk."

"But he was able to get it from the display onto the chair, or cart or whatever it was."

"Say, the stolen credit card number," said Mark. "Do you think this guy in Duluth could pinpoint exactly how his number was taken?"

"Hmm, I didn't ask him, but I can. I think you're onto something there. I don't know why I didn't think of it. Whoever took the number is either the thief or someone who can at least give us a direction."

"Exactly. But don't get your hopes up. Depending on how good he is with his records and how much he uses that card, it could be difficult to pinpoint exactly where the number was taken. It often is, especially if the person purchased anything online from a website. And if he purchased any kind of porn, well, then we'll never track down the identity thief."

"I'll get on it right now and get back to you," said Shaynah. "I've got a call scheduled with the credit card company anyway."

"I'm going to lunch. You want to come along?" Mark asked.

"Seriously?"

"Yeah, why? Can't I have lunch?"

"No," Shaynah replied, "it's not that. But I heard that you never have lunch with other people."

"I don't. But do you want to come or not?"

21

THE PAVLOVIAN INCIDENT

It was difficult for Zeke to work the day after he had sex with Craig. Craig kept smiling at him at the restaurant all day, and time could not move fast enough. He was an eighteen-year-old male who had never even masturbated before. Patience was not in his sexual vocabulary at this point.

During his two shifts that day, Zeke received $11.75 in cash tips. All his credit card tips would automatically go on his paycheck. At the end of the day, he opened the cash-tip locker and stood in front of the metal box that contained the cash. He was the only server left in the building. Craig had been home for hours, but one of the other managers was working in the office off the kitchen.

It would be pretty easy for me to take the money. It doesn't look like Karen has made a deposit in a while, and it wouldn't be hard to grab at least a couple hundred dollars. It wouldn't be missed. And Craig has a good point—it's a bad system. I am a really good server, and I should get more of a cut of the cash tips. But some of the other servers work hard, and they need money too. And even though it's a bad system, it's the system we have. Craig will understand. He's so nice to me. I really love him.

Zeke said goodbye to the manager on duty and left the restaurant. It was warm enough to be outside at night without even a coat. *I think we'll be able to go running without shirts tomorrow. Maybe my mom will see us. I wonder if I could get Craig to drive and go running in my parents' neighborhood.*

The thought of running with Craig gave him a lot of energy—a lot. He jumped in his car and raced back to the house. *How does this work? Do I just jump on him like I want to? Do I ask to have sex? I guess I don't care as long as it happens.* It seemed to take forever for him to get home. *Seriously, is this the most endless string of the longest red lights ever on the planet? It's going to feel so good. I hope it feels as good as last night. Craig said it would get even better each time.*

Zeke finally arrived in the driveway. He jumped out of the car. *Be cool.* He walked only slightly faster than usual to the door.

Craig was sitting on the couch, watching a show on the Investigation Discovery Network.

"Hey, Craig," Zeke said as he plopped next to Craig on the couch. "What've you been doing since you left work?" *Stupid thing to say.*

"I went for a run and mowed the lawn. It was nice out today. How was the evening shift?"

"Fine. Nothing eventful."

"What happened with the cash tips?"

Shoot. I was hoping he wouldn't get to that until much later. "Well," Zeke replied, "I just left it there. It didn't feel right. Is that okay? I mean, I get what you were saying to me, but it's just not me right now. But I'll pick up some extra shifts so that we can buy a bigger bed."

"Okay," Craig said. "No problem."

What should I do? He's probably waiting for me to make a move since he made the move last night. "How is the show you're watching?" Zeke asked.

"I've seen it before," Craig replied. "This guy makes a really stupid mistake. He kills that woman and then dips her finger in her own blood and uses it to write the name of her ex, in blood, on the wall.

So the cops get there and assume that she must have written that as she died, to tell everyone who did it. But the ex has a rock-solid alibi. So the cops investigate and find out that the woman is left-handed, but the blood was written with her right hand. That's when they track down the guy who really did it."

"He should have made sure he knew which hand she wrote with before trying something like that," said Zeke.

"Actually," Craig replied, "he shouldn't have done anything. Get in, do it, and get out. The more you think, the more you mess up. The ability to resist the temptation to waste time is the criminal's greatest ally. Don't forget that."

Well, Craig, if I ever commit a crime, I'll remember that. But I don't see that happening. I have to touch him so that he will touch me. I should just do it—jump right in and go for it. It's now or never. "Hey, Craig," Zeke said awkwardly, "is it okay if I put my hand on your knee?"

"Ah ... not right now," Craig replied. "I'm kind of into this episode even though I've seen it before." Then Craig got up from the couch and went and sat in Zeke's regular chair across the room.

What? Shoot. I can't believe it's not going to happen. Did I say something wrong? I have to know. "Are you okay?" Zeke asked.

"Oh yeah. I'm just going to finish this episode and then go to bed. I'm sort of tired. You working the evening shift again tomorrow night?"

"Yep."

"You the closing server?"

"Yep."

"Are you going to be alone when you close up the servers' lounge?"

"Yes, I guess. That's usually how it works. Why?"

"Oh, nothing. I'll see you when you get home."

What should I do? Just go to bed? Impossible.

Twenty-three hours later, Zeke once again stood in front of the metal cash-tip box inside the locker. *If anyone notices, they'll blame Dylan. People already suspect him of not putting in all his cash tips. And he's quitting anyway. He'll get the blame for sure. He even worked tonight. But nobody is going to notice if I leave a bigger bill on the top of the pile. Not even Karen will suspect anything.*

Zeke's mind was empty on the drive home. He was so consumed with the feeling of wanting to feel Craig's body on top of his that his brain wasn't capable of processing thoughts. He drove past Glensheen and didn't even think of the famous murders he'd been hearing about since childhood. After pulling into Craig's driveway and running through the door, Zeke threw his keys into the bowl on the counter. Then he plopped down next to Craig on the couch.

"Hey, how was work?" Craig asked.

"Same as usual. I got something for you." Zeke took a wad of cash out his back pocket and put it on Craig's lap.

Craig grabbed it and set it on a side table next to the couch.

"So how was your evening?" Zeke asked.

"Not eventful. Went running. Hey, Zeke, you can put your hand on my knee if you want."

22

THE INVESTIGATION SPLITS

Mark walked slowly down the hallway of the second floor of the Minnesota Bureau of Criminal Apprehension. It was an odd day for him. He'd never had a real work friend during his entire career. There had never been other gay men Mark's age around—they'd all died in the 1980s. Consequently, when he began his career, he had been the weird one because being in the closet had made him act oddly. Then he had been the weird one because he was the only openly gay person in his field. Now he was the weird one because he was a middle-aged gay man, and society wasn't sure what to do with that. However, today was odd for a different reason.

He approached Shaynah's open door, knocked on it, and entered her office. She was working at her computer, and he sat down on a chair next to her desk.

"Finishing up the final report?" he asked.

"Yep," Shaynah replied. "Almost done."

"I got your message last night that you were done with the investigation. I take it the credit card fraud didn't pan out?"

"Yeah, it's too bad. The victim of the fraud cooperated fully. But he used that credit card a lot. He'd also just become a widower before this whole thing started, so he's been eating at restaurants for every meal. Restaurants are the most likely places for complete card information to be taken, but he went to too many for me to even begin. So yeah, that's going to be about it. And since the thefts stopped when the media reported on them, well, this might be all we hear of it for a while. Hill has instructed me to move on."

"Will you get the report out to the museums?"

"Yes, as soon as it's approved. Marge down in Walnut Grove is already working on replacing the quilt. She's got some ladies sewing and even has a company reproducing the exact fabric patterns. Nobody cares about Lindbergh's plane—I think he's fallen out of favor a bit. The people in Sauk Centre are still hopeful that they will recover the Sinclair Lewis urn someday. Maybe they will. Who knows? As for the Kensington Runestone—"

"There are plenty of people," Mark interrupted, "who are actually happy that it's gone. I have a professor friend at Hamline University who told me he'd take credit for taking it if he could."

"Ha!" Shaynah laughed. "I've heard the same thing. A lot of people were embarrassed that the state even claimed that thing in the first place."

"We did send it to the World's Fair in '64. Maybe that makes it special enough?"

"Maybe. But of all the missing items, the runestone is the most likely to make an appearance at some point. It will be too hard to hide forever."

"Well," Mark continued, "Twin Cities Public Television wants to do a special about it. It makes a good story—missing artifacts from Minnesota museums. Director Hill wants to participate fully. I told her that you'll be great at working with the television folks. I said you'd be a natural in front of the camera. I look forward to seeing it."

"You don't want to be part of it?" Shaynah asked.

"Nope. Actually, Shaynah, I wanted you to hear it from me first. Today is my last day. I'm resigning today."

"What? This is a surprise. What's going on?" Shaynah asked with a concerned expression. "You're not retiring—I know that for sure. Did you get another job? Better pay?"

"Most people will assume that I'm old and retiring. I'm happy that you didn't jump to that conclusion. Really, thank you."

"Are you kidding? I know how much you love this stuff. I know that there is no way you are ready to retire. Something is going on, isn't it?"

"Yep. I … I haven't talked about my husband, Andrew, very much. And yes, Shaynah, I am calling him my husband because we got married."

"Well, it's about time. I'm so happy for you, but why wasn't I—"

"Let me finish. Andrew has had a tough time when it comes to work. He's not a good reader—never has been—and school was always tough for him. He didn't go to college. The last ten years, he's been selling kitchenware for one of those home marketing companies. He's actually really good at it—too good. But he never filed his taxes correctly.

"See, these pyramid-type companies are always giving free stuff. He was supposed to claim anything free he got from the company. He's gotten a lot of expensive trips and products over the years. He'd go to someone's house for a party, put on a show, and sell a bunch of stuff. Like I said, he's actually very good at it. So he's earned a lot of trips. We've been to Hawaii, California, Florida—all as incentives. But he's supposed to have treated all that free stuff like it was income. And to make it much worse, he never filed for the actual income he made.

"The IRS caught up with him. I couldn't let him handle this alone, so we got married. Now that he can prove some assets—my assets—he can avoid incarceration. We've made a payment plan with the IRS and Minnesota Revenue. But this all means that I can't work in law enforcement. I'll lose any kind of security clearance because I owe money to the IRS and was, basically, involved in tax fraud."

After a long pause, Shaynah said, "That's a beautiful thing to do. You must care for him an awful lot."

"I do. And it's partly my fault for not marrying him sooner, or at least for not paying more attention to his finances. I should have insisted on going over his paperwork with him. I know better and should have learned the tax laws with these pyramid companies. But when it all comes down to it, I know that there's no one else for me but him. I'm happy about that and ready to spend the rest of my life with him. He's worth it—giving all this up—and that makes me very happy."

"But you'll stay in touch, right?"

"I've never had friends around here, and I really don't need any. But I wouldn't mind meeting for lunch once in a while."

23

STEALING FROM THE FATHER

Zeke's dad was the pastor of a create-your-own-denomination Christian church. He was the only employee. Larger operations had a businessperson who oversaw the church's money. But in Pastor Smith's case, he was the whole affair.

Each Sunday, Smith gathered all the donations into a metal lockbox. He brought the box home and then took it to the bank on Monday to make a deposit. But Zeke knew that he always took a bit of the cash and hid it in a closet at the Smith home. Zeke had found it once. There was several thousand dollars of cash hidden in a cardboard box underneath two sweaters that were way too small for the pastor to wear.

On a Wednesday night two weeks after he'd stolen from the cash tips at the restaurant, Zeke drove to his old neighborhood and parked on his parents' driveway. Wednesday night was church night. *None of the family will be home. Nobody will recognize my car, but even if they see me, my dad can't do anything. He's not going to take the chance of accusing me of stealing money that he already stole. I hope my key still works.*

It didn't. *They changed the locks. They really must not want me back.* But Zeke knew that his parents always kept a key hidden under a statue of an angel that sat among a bed of overgrown ferns in the backyard. *So predictable. Hiding a safety key under a guardian angel.* The key worked, and Zeke entered his former home through the back door. *They changed the lock, but they didn't change the hiding spot for the extra key. I can hear my mom saying that the angel will always protect the key—she didn't even give me a second thought.*

It was quiet in the house. *Sort of eerie in here. I kind of like it. It feels like there are all these emotions hanging around in the air, and only I can feel them.*

He went to his parents' bedroom and opened the closet door. He retrieved the cardboard box from way in the back. When he opened it, he discovered a lot more cash than he had remembered or anticipated. *God, there's a lot of money in here. Thousands! I'll have to take the whole box.* Zeke took the sweaters out of the box and put them on the bed. Then he took a few moments to lay the sweaters out, so that it looked like two men were holding hands on the bed.

He walked through the rest of the house, carrying the cardboard box. *Maybe I should hide a stash of money for one of the kids to find. Never mind. They'll need to make their own way.*

Back in the kitchen, before leaving through the back door, he noticed an item on the counter that made him instantly stop. He abruptly slammed the box on the kitchen table, walked over to the counter, and picked up a cloth apron. *Grandma's old apron. Mom is still using it, though still not ever for cooking. One of the kids must have pissed her off before the family went to church. God, I remember the times I bent over that chair, my bare ass sticking up, as she twisted it into a tight rope and whipped me like guys did with their towels in the locker room—always telling us that Jesus was not happy with us until we bled like he did. There's even fresh blood stains on it now. I'm going to take it home and wash it. I'll use it to bake cookies for the man I'm having sex with—having sex with and enjoying it. I'll use Grandma's apron for that.*

Zeke grabbed the apron and stuck it in the cardboard box. Then

MICHAEL FRIDGEN

he left the house without locking the door. He threw the spare key out into the middle of the lawn and pushed over the angel. It fell, and one of its wings broke off. *They'll never report anything. They'll know it was me, but what can they do when Dad has been stealing all this money over the years?*

As he drove away, he breathed deeply. *God, that felt good! I'm leaving them forever. I'm going back to a man who loves me and takes care of me. I get to spend my life with Craig, and they get to go to church. I win.*

For almost an entire year, Zeke committed acts of petty theft under Craig's guidance. They hit most stores in the area, taking small items and clothing. Zeke got good at attending church services and stealing from the collection baskets. At times Craig was frustrated that they couldn't get anything bigger. But he was patient and realized the importance of that patience.

Craig bought a king-size bed for his bedroom. To his surprise, he liked having someone else to sleep with. He liked that Zeke was close to him most of the time. He found it easier to fake the enjoyment of sex with each crime he could get Zeke to commit. Craig got off on the power. Zeke got off on all the sex.

They also spent the year watching true crime on television. Craig was obsessed with stories of criminals and their trials. Zeke didn't have a choice in the matter—it was all he was able to watch as well. Night after night, after their shifts at the restaurant, they sat on the couch and dissected whatever crime they were watching.

When they weren't watching true crime, they were planning for real crime. Craig showed Zeke the supply cabinet in the basement. They practiced using handcuffs, zip ties, injectable drugs, and countless physical skills. Craig developed a rigorous schedule that involved running, lifting weights, and rehearsing crime scenarios. It was a year of obsession.

The summer in northern Minnesota was gorgeous, with weather

better than that of Southern California. It just didn't last very long. By the end of August, a beautiful but short autumn had begun. And then came the long cold winter. Once Lake Superior froze, it acted like a giant ice cube sitting in the lap of every Duluthian. It took until early May for that ice cube to entirely melt. Then spring was finally back.

Their year of petty theft, working out, true crime television, and sex was coming to an end. Both men wanted more. Craig wanted more power. Zeke wanted more sex that he thought was love.

MICHAEL FRIDGEN

PART II

24

ANOTHER MESSY TABLE

Geno's Restaurant was founded in 1935 by an Italian family living in Duluth. In 1973, a second location opened next to the brand-new Miller Hill Mall. The restaurants were widely popular until they declined, along with most of Duluth, in the 1980s due to the weakening iron ore industry. The original downtown Geno's closed in 1993. The mall location went through several owners until it was purchased by Karen O'Neil in 2001. From that time until now, the restaurant had gone through cycles of ups and downs—depending on Karen's priorities and ability to focus on numbers.

It was another spring in Duluth. Many Duluthians were out and about, wearing shorts and tank tops in weather that would make Floridians break out their parkas. Zeke's body had changed since he graduated from high school the previous spring. He was now nineteen, an age when genetics and hormones made it possible to easily add muscle. He'd also been under Craig's tutelage for a year, with plenty of running and hardly any junk food. Zeke's face wasn't as handsome as Craig's, but his body turned many heads when he ran around the University of Minnesota Duluth campus.

During the entire year, Zeke had seen his parents only once, at the grocery store. They had ignored him and fled the store, leaving their full shopping cart in the middle of an aisle. He'd laughed.

Craig had started attending Pastor Smith's Sunday service once each month at the Lake Superior Celebration Church. He always told Zeke he was going for a drive and some alone time. Craig loved hearing the preacher go on and on about how to live a virtuous life—all the while knowing that he'd turned his son into a delinquent. Craig made sure to shake the pastor's hand at the end of each service. Once, Craig put a pair of Zeke's used underwear in the collection basket when no one was watching.

But working at the restaurant was starting to become a drain on Craig's spirit. It was just too ordinary for him. *If I want to quit this place, I'll need a lot more money. We've got to step things up. We need cash—untraceable cash from unsuspecting people. Credit card fraud is too risky, and it's impossible to liquidate stolen goods. We're going to start soon, and we're going to start with cash.*

It was the Sunday before Memorial Day. Craig and Zeke were both working the busy lunch shift. Craig was in the back, helping the cooks by organizing supplies on the counters. He didn't mind this task—at least it was better than sitting in the office and working on the schedule. From where he was working, he could see into the dining room through a window in the swinging kitchen door. He watched as Zeke continued to serve a high-maintenance table. Eventually, Zeke bounded through the swinging door with a loud sigh and a small plate of spaghetti.

"Rough table?" Craig said without looking up from a large box of dried pasta.

"The roughest," Zeke replied.

"What do they want now?" asked one of the two cooks as she walked over and grabbed the plate from Zeke.

"Yeah, can you put some shredded cheddar cheese on this?"

"You mean parmesan?" asked the cook.

"No, I mean shredded cheddar," Zeke replied.

"Whatever," said the cook.

"You know," Craig said, "I was watching a documentary about this murder in Japan. A flight attendant for British Airways was killed by this weird guy who hacked up her body."

"What in the hell does that have to do with this spaghetti?" laughed the other cook. "You're always coming up with stuff like this."

"I'm getting to that," said Craig. "I learned in this documentary that it's very, very rude in Japan to ask for a special accommodation at a restaurant. They see it as being very disrespectful to the people who work at the place. How did this whole thing get started in the US? How did we get to this place where people think they can just get whatever they want whenever they want?"

"I think it was McDonald's," replied the second cook. "They said I could always have it my way. But now we're all stuck doing it. If you don't accommodate, you lose business."

"Well, whatever," said Zeke. "Just do it fast because that dad out there is a tyrant, and I'm tired of it."

"I'll take it out," said Craig. He grabbed the small plate of spaghetti, now covered with shredded cheddar, and went through the door into the dining room. He walked up to the table where the mom, dad, and two toddlers sat. The parents were both in their thirties.

"Here you go," said Craig as he set the plate in front of the kid who didn't have one. "How does that look?"

"It's looks terrible," said the dad. "Way too much cheese."

"Oh, let him eat it," said the mom. "He'll starve before they get it right."

"We're not paying for that," said the dad. "You'd think that spaghetti would be pretty easy to get right."

"I'm sorry about that," Craig replied. *What an asshole. I hope he threatens never to come back here.*

"You will be sorry," the dad continued. "We are never coming back here again."

No! Say it isn't so! "I'm sorry to hear that," said Craig.

"We drove all this way to shop and eat," said the mom. "I guess we should've stayed in Hibbing, where they know how to make a kid's spaghetti."

Hibbing! I was raised in that shithole. Nobody in that town has ever had spaghetti that didn't come from a can with a cartoon on it.

Craig took a step back and noticed the floor under the table. It was full of crackers, cheerios, and a juice box that had been ripped open and spilled. *I hate these people, especially since they are from Hibbing. I wonder how much money this asshole keeps in the house.*

"I'll tell you what," said Craig. "I'm sorry you've had such a bad time here. Your lunch is on me. Why don't you just enjoy the drive back to Hibbing? It's a nice day."

"That's the best thing I've heard all morning," said the mom. "Let's head back."

"I'm still not coming back here," said the dad. "This place should pay people to eat here."

Craig left the table and went back into the kitchen.

"Everything okay?" Zeke asked.

"Yep. They're going to leave. I took care of it. But hey, can you guys hold down the place until Shari gets here? I want to leave a little early today—it'll be just for an hour or so. I need a break. I'll call Shari and let her know."

"No problem," said one of the cooks. "Have a good afternoon."

Zeke followed him into the manager's office and said, "Are you sure you're okay?"

"I'm fine, seriously. I just want to go for a long run. I'll be home when you get home tonight."

"Well, thanks for taking care of that table. That dad was a real something else."

"Asshole. Yes, he was. But I'm taking care of it, and I'll see you tonight."

25

IT'S THEIR TIME

That same day, Zeke was finishing his shift as the closing server when his phone rang. It was Craig. He walked back into a storeroom and answered.

"Hey," Zeke said. "Are you okay?"

"Yeah, we're going ahead with our plan tonight."

"Tonight?"

"Yep. So as soon as you're done, drive straight home. Leave your car in the driveway. Go inside and put on all your blacks. Don't forget the shoes. Grab the supply satchel from the planning supply closet—I already put the supplies in there. Remember to leave your phone on the kitchen counter next to mine. Don't forget about the phone; you don't want it with you. Then make sure the doors are locked and run out on the back trail. Go through to the park. I'll meet you in a blue rental car in the lot by the picnic shelter."

"Sounds good." *Yes! Finally, we are going to do something big. He's going to be so worked up afterward. This is going to be great—I can't wait.*

Zeke ended the call and said goodbye to the night manager. He jumped in his car and proceeded exactly as Craig had instructed. His brain was in a heightened state of processing. He didn't forget about the shoes or to leave his phone on the counter. He locked the doors, checked that nobody else was around, and started running toward the back path. It was dark.

Zeke reached the park and waited in the darkness at the picnic shelter for about forty minutes. It seemed like an eternity. *I hope nothing is wrong. If I mess up, I can say I'm sorry. But if he messes up, then he'll be in a really bad mood. I want him in a good mood after all this is done.*

Zeke had just about reached the point of anxiety when headlights approached the picnic shelter, from a vehicle coming down a narrow park road. *It has to be him. It's too late for anyone else to be out.* A blue car approached. Zeke saw Craig waving through the driver's side window. He grabbed the satchel and got into the car.

"Where are we going?" Zeke asked as they drove out of the park.

"Hibbing."

"Hibbing? Where you're from? I've never been there, even though it's so close."

"Well, you're not missing much. But this isn't for me. This is work. Got it?"

"Of course. But how did you decide what house we're going for?"

"It's the home of the asshole guy and his family from the restaurant today," said Craig.

"Seriously? How did you find them?" Zeke asked.

"I followed them all the way to Hibbing this afternoon."

"That's awesome—they deserve it. I had to clean up all that shit they left on the floor."

"Yeah, well, don't let that get in the way of the plan. We get in, do our thing, and get out. I'll take the gun and be on control duty. You'll take the knife and be on acquisition duty. We want cash—that's it. Leave anything else that looks valuable. It's too hard to sell any of that. And no trophies for yourself. The more things you touch in the house, the more chance of leaving a trail. We get in and get out. Got it?"

"Yes, I got it. I've been thinking about this for months, just like you. I've got it all down."

"What if the kids start crying?" Craig asked.

"Doesn't matter. Not our concern. I told you, I got this." *I really do have it all down. It's going to be perfect, and then we'll head home, and we'll go to bed. He'll be so worked up that we'll go at it all night. And then we'll fall asleep together and sleep in real late. That's my favorite part—sleeping in real late and talking in bed.*

"How long is the drive?" Zeke asked. "An hour?"

"It's just a little under two hours. I'm not going to speed in either direction—not with a gun in the satchel."

They didn't say anything else on the drive. Because of his sheltered upbringing, Zeke hadn't been out of Duluth very much. He was surprised at how dark it was on the highway. The stars were extremely bright. There was no moon.

After an hour and forty-two minutes, Zeke saw a sign welcoming them to Hibbing, Minnesota, home of Bob Dylan.

"You know," said Craig, "Bob Dylan won the Nobel Prize for Literature. Two Minnesotans have won that prize. The other was Sinclair Lewis. Ever heard of him?"

"No," Zeke answered. *Why is he smirking at me like that? Should I know about Sinclair Lewis?*

After just a few more minutes of silence, Craig turned into a residential neighborhood and parked the car along the side of a street. "Okay," said Craig, "when I open the door, no more talking until we get inside. You got it? You got the plan?"

"Yes, don't worry about me."

Craig grabbed the satchel and looked inside. He retrieved two black nylon face masks and gave one to Zeke. They put on their respective masks, and Craig gave Zeke a thumbs-up, signaling that he could see okay. Zeke returned the gesture. Then Craig took two small headbands from the satchel, each with a tiny LED light on it. He gave one to Zeke, and they put their headbands on.

Zeke saw Craig take one last look in the bag. *Yes,* Zeke thought, *I double-checked—the gun, knife, and zip ties are in there. No need to always check my work. But I guess he cares enough to want everything to be perfect.*

Craig opened his door, got out, and closed it softly. Zeke did the same, closing his door without a sound. Then Craig took off running alongside a house, through a backyard, and into a grove of trees. Zeke easily stayed with him the entire time, even though Craig was running briskly. Aside from the occasional crack of a twig or brush of a leaf, they were extremely quiet.

Zeke followed Craig through a couple more backyards. *I hope he checked all these yards for cameras. Oh well, it probably won't matter because we're not showing any skin. I wonder how well he knows this town anyway. We're in great shape. I'm not breathing hard, and he isn't either. The training is really going to make the difference for us.*

Craig turned, ran around some trees, and entered the dark backyard of an older home. Zeke noticed that the detached garage had peeling paint, but it was too dark to get a good look at the actual home. He stopped next to Craig when they got to a back door. Craig reached into his side pocket and took out his universal lock pick. He turned toward Zeke. Zeke couldn't make out anything on his face but knew that this was Craig's way of telling him there was no turning back.

God, I hope the pick works, Zeke thought as he watched Craig work. *Thank God—it did!*

Craig opened the door and touched the LED light on his head. A single bright beam shone straight into a kitchen. Zeke followed him and turned on his light. They walked silently through the kitchen and stopped when they entered a living room. All was quiet. Zeke noticed the front door and saw a wood plaque above it that said "Welcome to The Kearneys'." *The Kearneys. That's their name. Oh, Craig already has the gun out.* Then Craig reached into the satchel and gave Zeke the knife.

Zeke followed Craig up a straight flight of stairs. They climbed slowly, but the steps still creaked every once in a while. At the top of the stairs, an open door was directly in front of them. Craig's light revealed that it was a small bathroom. They walked down a dark hall and peered into the first room that they came to. Inside, Zeke saw two beds in the shape of race cars. He looked in, attempting to focus his light. But Craig started closing the door before he got a chance to see the sleeping kids. After Craig closed the door, they continued down the hall.

There was only one more door, at the end of the corridor. It was open. Craig stepped in first, and Zeke followed close behind. They turned their heads to get a good look at the room. It was a normal master bedroom with one interior door. *That must be a closet,* thought Zeke. *They don't have their own bathroom. Shit, they probably don't have too much cash. I hope we get something, or Craig might be pissed. But look at them sleeping on that bed. They have no idea that they're about to be afraid. I wonder how—*

Craig switched on the overhead light in the bedroom. Zeke's eyes adjusted quickly. The mom sat up first and looked stunned for a split second. Then she took a deep breath and opened her mouth to scream, but nothing came out.

"What?" she eventually said. "What's going on?"

The dad finally stirred. He opened his eyes, took a moment to really understand that two men dressed all in black were in his bedroom, and jumped out of the bed. The mom started whimpering and getting louder.

"Okay," said Craig calmly, pointing the gun at Mrs. Kearney, "nobody move. And nobody scream. We don't want to wake your kids. There's no sense in scaring them."

"What do you want?" said Mr. Kearney. "You can have anything you want—just leave us alone."

"We want cash," said Craig.

"I don't have much in the house, but you can have everything I have."

"Here's how this works," said Craig. "Mom, you're going to stay in bed, and I'm going to stay with you. Dad, you're going to go with my friend here and get all the cash. Don't try anything because I'll be up here with this gun on your wife. Now everyone is going to be fine, I promise. So let's get moving and get this over with. And do it all nice and quiet so we don't wake up the kids."

Zeke motioned to the door with his knife. Craig retrieved some zip ties from the satchel and handed them to Zeke.

"My wallet's downstairs," said Mr. Kearney.

"I'll follow you," said Zeke. *My voice sounds weird. I like it.*

Zeke followed the man down the hall without looking back at Craig. The man paused slightly in front of the closed door to his kids' bedroom and then went immediately down the stairs. Zeke stayed right behind him. *He looks the same, but he's a totally different person than the guy in the restaurant. He even talks differently. He was such an alpha male this afternoon, and now he seems like a nothing. He's a lot uglier too.*

Mr. Kearney led Zeke to a small room off of the living room and opposite the kitchen. It was a laundry room. The man grabbed his wallet from the top of a front-loading washing machine. He reached in, pulled out two bills, and gave them to Zeke.

Forty bucks! "Forty bucks?" said Zeke. "That's it? That's all you have, forty bucks?"

"Honestly, man, I use credit cards for everything," Mr. Kearney replied. "You have to believe me."

"There has to be more. You must have some emergency cash somewhere. In a desk somewhere? What about your wife? She must have a purse. I can't believe you'd have two kids in a house—yes, I know you have two kids—with just forty bucks. What if there was a blizzard and the power went off at the grocery store? How would you pay?"

"My wife's purse is right there on the dryer. Look through it, but there's nothing in it. Honestly, man, you have to believe me. We went shopping today. She gave this forty dollars to me this afternoon. I have a bunch of emergency cash in my office—I mean, my actual office, an insurance office in town—not here at the house. I'm being completely honest with you, man. Just leave us alone, and we won't even call the cops."

I think he's telling the truth about the cash. He seems like it. But he's lying about not calling the cops. He'll call the cops as soon as he gets a chance. Should we take him with us to his office? No, that's not in the plan. And the more places we go, the more chances to leave a trail. Shit! This whole thing is going south. Craig is going to flip over just forty bucks! This is going to wreck everything.

"Okay," said Zeke. "Just get on your knees." *Follow through with the plan regardless. Tie him up. We got in, and now we need to get out. Follow the plan. Tie them up so that we have more time to get away.*

"I'm not doing that," said Mr. Kearney.

"Yes, you are, if you want your wife and kids to be safe. My friend's up there with a gun, remember? One yell, and it's over. Now get on your knees and face the washing machine."

Mr. Kearney nodded slightly and did as Zeke instructed.

"Put your hands behind your back." *I love the way my voice sounds when I say that.*

Zeke shoved all of the zip ties except one into his pants pocket. He set the knife on the dryer. *That wasn't in the plan. But we didn't think about how I'd use the zip ties with only one hand. We'll have to talk about that.* Zeke took the zip tie and tied Mr. Kearney's hands together behind his back. Then he took another tie from his pocket and bound the man's feet together. Mr. Kearney remained on his knees, saying nothing. *I hope Craig's got the mom tied up so that we can get out of here.*

The man started whimpering a little. Then he was fully crying.

Damn. He's crying. That's messed up. A grown man crying, a man who treated me like crap this afternoon and left all sorts of shit for me to clean up on the floor. And now he's crying in front of me. I did that. For forty bucks! For forty—

Zeke's mind suddenly went blank. He began to move swiftly without any emotion. He reached into his pocket and pulled out another zip tie. He put it around Mr. Kearney's throat. The man started to thrash around, but he wasn't strong enough with his limbs tied together. Zeke pressed him into the linoleum floor, then grabbed either end of the zip tie again. He pulled as hard as he could with both hands. The long industrial tie locked tighter with each click. *I love the sound of the clicks.*

At first, there was gasping. Then Mr. Kearney shook violently in short bursts. Finally, after a period that seemed much longer than it really was, there was nothing. Zeke bent down and tightened the tie as much as he possibly could. The man's face started to turn blue. Zeke stood up, grabbed the knife, and looked down at him. He was still. Zeke bent down and turned him over. His eyes and mouth were open, but his eyeballs weren't moving. There wasn't any blinking.

Craig's probably wondering what's taking so long. He won't come down to check on me—that's not the plan. The plan.

Zeke made sure he had the knife and the two twenty-dollar bills that he'd stuck in his back pocket. He checked that he hadn't dropped anything on the floor. Then he went upstairs and into the master bedroom. Craig had tied up Mrs. Kearney with the zip ties. She looked terrified.

"We all good?" Craig asked.

"Yeah," Zeke replied. "He's in the laundry room—tied up."

"Okay, Mom," said Craig. "See, I told you we weren't going to hurt anyone."

He doesn't know. He won't like it.

"So," Craig continued, "we're going now. Just stay nice and quiet for a good hour. Then you can do whatever you want to get some help. The kids will sleep through it."

Craig turned and walked out of the bedroom, switching off the light as he passed it. Zeke followed him down the hall and to the stairs.

"You need me to check on the dad to make sure he's secure?" Craig asked.

"Nah, he's good." *What am I going to do? I have to tell him. I'm in over my head on this one, and I'll need him to think it over so that we're safe. I'll tell him in the car, not now.*

26

THE BEST-LAID PLANS
OF MAN AND MAN

They ran silently back the way they had come toward the car. Zeke followed closely behind Craig. They stayed silent as they got into the car. Then, while they both kept their masks on, Craig checked that they had the gun and the knife in the satchel. He gave Zeke a thumbs-up. They both took off their headband lights and masks and put everything in the satchel. Craig looked at Zeke and noticed that he was pale and pasty. *I guess that's to be expected. Poor kid. I'll make it up to him tonight. I hope we got a lot.*

Craig started the car and pulled away from the residential area. They hit the highway, and Craig turned on the cruise control—three miles per hour below the speed limit. It was almost 2:45 a.m. "Okay," said Craig, breaking the silence, "you did good. Everything went according to the plan. How much did we get?"

Zeke was silent. He stared straight ahead at the highway.

"Well?" Craig asked again.

"Forty dollars," Zeke said in a robotic tone.

Forty dollars? Did I hear that right? I must have. He looks terrible. "Forty dollars? Seriously?" said Craig.

"Yeah."

He didn't try hard enough. I should have done acquisition, and he should have been control. "You didn't try hard enough. There had to have been more."

"Nope. He keeps his money at his insurance office somewhere in town. Forty dollars is it."

"He knew you were going soft. We'll switch the next time. I'll take acquisition, and you'll have to get some guts to be the control."

"Craig, I killed him," Zeke said.

"Yeah, you killed him all right. That's why you got all that cash to show for it."

"No, Craig, I mean I really killed him. He's dead."

What? Did he really just say that? "What? You serious? What the hell is going on?"

Craig stopped the car abruptly. The tires squealed. Zeke continued to stare straight ahead as Craig pulled the car over onto the side of the highway. Then Craig turned and smacked Zeke hard on the face. Zeke didn't react, except to turn and face the passenger-side window.

"You're serious! What the hell, Zeke! Christ! What happened? Tell me!"

"I don't know, Craig. I mean, I really don't know how—what happened. He had two twenties in his wallet. The wife's purse was there with nothing. He told me about the cash at his office. Then I had him get on his knees, just how we'd practiced at home. I tied up his hands and feet. Then—I don't know why—I put a zip tie around his neck and tightened it. Tight. He died. I saw his eyes."

Christ. He's telling the truth. He actually killed the bastard. What the hell is wrong with him? "Do you know what you've done?" Craig asked harshly as he struck Zeke again. "This isn't just some theft anymore. This is bad. You killed someone—and there's a body. A body is a ton of forensic evidence. Haven't you learned anything from me? I really had high hopes for you. We've planned and watched so much TV about this. You left a body! A big old sack of blood and DNA that tells a story. I can't believe you've done this to us. You've ruined us.

We can't have a relationship now. Zeke, you have ruined everything. And you fucking killed someone! Christ! I'm not a killer, Zeke. I'm a lot of things, but I am not a killer. I am not someone who could physically hurt another person—that was my dad. I am not my dad." *You have to get it together and start driving. You are in way too much trouble to be sitting alongside a highway. Just get back to Duluth. Get it together to get home.* Craig put the car into drive and headed down the highway. *Be especially careful—do not speed. So much for having an accomplice.*

"Okay," said Craig after several minutes, "no talking until we get home. We have to return the car tonight and put the keys in the drop box. Then we'll run to where I left my car. We won't forget the satchel. They'll clean the car. But it's a good thing you strangled him. There was no blood, right?" He waited a moment for Zeke to answer. "Zeke—no blood, right? You didn't use the knife, right?"

"No, there wasn't any blood," Zeke said, still looking out the side window. "I used the zip tie, like I told you."

"Did he tear your clothes or touch your skin at all?"

"No, he didn't have a chance."

"Did you ever take your gloves off?"

"Of course not."

"We need to get rid of our shoes. There's probably footprints. Christ, I almost forgot—we have to put the correct plates back on the car." *Shit, I can't forget these things.* "No more talking—just let me think."

They were about twenty miles from Duluth, still driving slightly below the speed limit. Periodically, Craig looked over, but Zeke never changed position. He remained slumped against the passenger-side door, with his face just a few inches from the window.

"You're not going to throw up, are you?" Craig asked.

Zeke didn't say anything but shook his head briefly.

"Don't throw up. We don't need any extra DNA in here. And we don't need the car company pissed off."

I've been to Hibbing and back two times in one day. That's twice as much as I've been there over the last twenty years. I hate that damn town. And now I really hate that damn town. But if I was going to be involved in a homicide, I guess Hibbing is the town where I would have chosen for it to happen. Maybe he did me a favor. But probably not—definitely not.

He won't be able to forget that face. I can't forget seeing Dad's dead face with his eyes open. I came home from school, and there he was on the couch—dead. Did I drop my backpack? I can't remember. I remember calling 911 and the operator asking me how old I was. I said twelve instead of thirteen because I was shocked at seeing him, and I forgot how old I really was. I wonder if the trailer is still there. I could've gone and looked, but I doubt I'll ever go back to Hibbing now. I hope I never have to go back to Hibbing. I hope I don't have to face charges and be on trial for murder. Christ! What a mess.

I need to turn him in. I can't live like this. It will eat me up—always wondering if we're going to get caught. If they investigate now, they'll find the evidence to prove that I'm telling the truth. But the longer it goes, the greater the chance that I'll be implicated in the actual act. I was upstairs the whole time, tying up the mom. I'll probably get prison time, but maybe I'll make a deal. I can handle a few years—it will be much better than living with the uncertainty.

I lived with a bit of fear that they'd track me down for the stuff I stole from the museums. But there's a big difference between facing a theft charge and facing murder. What was going on in his head? He's way more messed up than I thought. All the religion, probably. There's no way I could've messed him up that much.

Craig looked for the satchel and saw it sitting on the seat beside Zeke. There was plenty of room for it on the seat with Zeke still curled up by the window. Craig reached into the satchel with his right hand, felt for the gun, and retrieved it. He drove with his left hand and kept the gun in his right hand.

"So, Zeke," Craig said, breaking the long silence.

Zeke didn't look at him.

"I've been thinking, and I want to tell you that I'm going to turn you in."

"What?" Zeke said as he quickly turned his head toward Craig. "What?"

"I can't live like this, with what you did and the part I had in it. I just can't. I don't want to. That's not the life I want for myself."

"You can't do that—turn me in. Like you said, there's no DNA evidence."

"It's impossible to not leave at least some sort of clue. Maybe they'll find a way to track the car. I don't know. But I can't live with the waiting. I want you to get your stuff and get out of the house. I'll give you an hour so that you'll have a chance to get away, if you want. Take the car and all your stuff."

"Where am I supposed to go? What about us?"

"I don't know where you should go. Canada is closer, but Mexico is easier to get lost in. You're young. You should probably go to another state and start new. Get rid of the car as fast as you can. Take one of the stolen credit cards and use it to take the train somewhere. You'll have to live in a crappy motel for a while, but eventually you can start to rebuild a life. You can take the money in the emergency pile—it's in the planning supply closet."

"But I love you. You can't get rid of me."

"Zeke, you don't love me. You just think you do. We don't have love; we have sex. You're too young to know the difference." *Should I tell him that I'm not even gay? Probably not. It might put him over the edge.*

"What about our other plans? The other jobs? All the money we were going to get and then move to Mexico or South America and have a big house? What about all of that?"

"Zeke, my mind is made up. I'm giving you an hour starting when we pull into the driveway. What you do with the hour is your choice, but you'll have an hour. Then I'm calling the police."

27

DR. KELLERMAN'S MONSTER

For the first time, Zeke felt the crushing blow of being pushed out by someone he was deeply in love with. Unfortunately, it was occurring at the same time that he was dealing with the fallout of having killed someone.

How can he do this to me? We were supposed to stay together forever. What about moving to the Mexican Riviera? We were going to have so much money that we could move there and live without being afraid of being caught. I'm never going to have sex with him again, and I can't face that. I can't accept that. I have to have sex with him. I have to sleep with him. I can't not feel his body. I know every muscle and feel of him, the smell of him. I have to feel him.

They drove through Duluth's only real suburb, Hermantown, and passed the Miller Hill Mall. Zeke saw the sign for Geno's glowing in the early morning darkness. *The sun will start coming up soon. I wish I could either go back one night or go forward a whole year. I don't want to feel this way.*

When they got to the rental car place, Zeke followed Craig robotically. Craig grabbed the satchel, still holding the gun in his hand.

Zeke knew that Craig used this particular place because it was small and shoddy and didn't have any cameras.

Zeke watched as Craig took a long and careful look all over the car. He took two license plates that were sitting on the back seat. Awkwardly, because he was still holding the gun and had the satchel flung around him, Craig used a small screwdriver from his pocket to change the plates. Then he placed the substitute plates in his satchel and put the rental car keys into the drop box. Without looking at Zeke, Craig took off at a brisk jog. Zeke followed until they came to Craig's car, parked on the side of a wooded road on the edge of town. *The next stop is home. What should I do?*

They started their drive toward home. With every turn, they got closer to the house. Zeke's anxiety went up. *Why did he take the gun from the satchel? He doesn't trust me. Why should he? I killed a man for no reason. I guess I'd take the gun too. I could still stab him with the knife if I could get it. What the hell is wrong with me?*

The house came into view. Craig pulled into the driveway, maneuvered around Zeke's car, and drove into the garage. "You have one hour," Craig said.

Stop saying that! What the hell is wrong with you? I can't just—

"Zeke, did you hear me? Are you listening? You have an hour."

"Yes," Zeke replied softly, "I heard you." *What should I do?*

Craig grabbed the satchel, took the house keys from the car's cup holder, and got out of the car. He unlocked the door that led from the garage into the house and stepped inside.

Zeke sat alone in the car. He stayed there for several minutes, wondering what Craig was doing inside. *Maybe he'll come out with a couple of suitcases. He'll say that we're going to go together to Mexico. We'll live together like those two guys from the Shawshank Redemption. He's not coming out. I'll have to go in.*

Zeke opened the car door slowly and crawled out of the car. He felt tired and just wanted to go to bed. He went into the house. Craig was sitting at the kitchen table. The satchel and gun were on the table in front of him. *He's not packing his suitcase. I hope he turns and looks at me.* But Craig didn't.

Maybe I'll take the money and go but stay in Duluth. I can use a stolen credit card and get a hotel somewhere. I'll find a way to see Craig. I can shave my head. Zeke walked down a short hall and opened the door that led to the basement. After walking down the stairs, he crossed an unfinished space and approached a large standing cabinet. *The planning supply closet—I love that he has formal names for this stuff, like "the person on control" and "the person on acquisition." I guess I didn't do a very good job at that.*

Zeke opened the cabinet and looked for a metal lockbox on the top shelf. *Wait. I don't have to go anywhere. I can stay here. I just need some time to convince him. He's upset, but he'll come around. I need time.*

Zeke stared at a small cardboard box sitting on a shelf at eye level. He opened the box. *Cat valium—ketamine. We were going to use these in a future robbery.* He took two syringes preloaded with liquid from the box. *I'll use one and then another one if I need to.*

Zeke dropped everything else he had and stomped straight up the stairs. Craig was still sitting at the kitchen table, his back to the entrance into the living room. Both men were still wearing their black clothes. Zeke walked past the couch. He placed one syringe in his back pocket and flicked the cap off the other. *Craig made me practice on an orange. But this time I only get one chance. He's very strong. I'll need to be fast. Commit and do it.* The gun was still lying on top of the satchel on the kitchen table, within easy reach of Craig's hand.

Without saying anything, Zeke moved quickly behind Craig and stabbed him in the upper arm with the syringe. He pressed on the plunger as hard as he could. The stretchy black fabric of his shirt had been easy to penetrate. Craig grabbed the gun and tried to turn around in his chair.

How long does it take? Zeke wondered. He shoved Craig as hard as he could. Craig fell to the floor but managed to keep holding onto the gun. Immediately, Zeke flung his body on top of Craig's. Craig was attempting, with great force, to roll over. Zeke kept him pinned. *He's so strong. He has the gun, but he can't point it. He's losing strength. How much longer? It can't take that long.*

Craig's movements became slow. He was trying to talk, but the sounds coming out of his mouth didn't sound like words. Eventually, Craig wasn't able to hold on to the gun, and he let it rest under his hand on the floor. Zeke knocked the gun away with his right hand, and it scooted across the kitchen floor. Then he turned Craig over. *His eyes are barely open. That's a good sign.* Zeke put his right ear against Craig's chest. He wrapped his arms around him and hugged tightly. *That feel so good. He's still breathing. He's going to be fine. How long does the cat valium last? I think he told me, but I don't remember. Probably a couple of hours. There's no landline anymore in the house, and both our phones are still on the kitchen counter. I'll have to stop hugging him to get the zip ties from downstairs and the good hand-cuffs—two sets. I could hug him forever.*

28

ZEKE'S DELUSION OF GRANDEUR

Climbing back through the fog took considerable time and effort. Craig drifted in and out, more in than out with each waking. And each time he grasped new sensations that he had to realize were real and not imagined. He needed to learn to trust that his eyes were seeing. When his brain finally broke the last barrier, he saw that he was in his basement. But he was lying on a mattress. *I don't have a mattress in the basement. How did it get here? How did I get here? This is my basement.*

There was a strain on his right arm. He tried to move it and noticed that he was handcuffed to the home's main sewer pipe. *I'm cold.* He realized that he was not alone. Zeke was lying next to him on the mattress. *I'm only wearing boxers—that's why I'm cold. Shit. My head hurts, and everything else hurts. This idiot has completely lost his mind. Something must have snapped in that house in Hibbing. I guess I created a monster. I wanted his dad to be disappointed—I accomplished that. I have to get out of this. How tight are the handcuffs? Shit, these are the professional-grade cuffs that cost a fortune. I'll never get—*

"Oh, hey," said Zeke as he rolled over to face him. "You're awake. I thought you'd sleep all day, and you almost did."

"What time is it?" Craig asked.

"I think it's like two in the afternoon."

"What's going on?"

"Listen, Craig, I'm sorry about the ketamine," said Zeke.

The ketamine. That was it—I really did create a monster. We practiced with the ketamine on oranges. He's been learning from everything I've been saying. This isn't going to be too good for me.

"I really am sorry," Zeke continued. "It was the only way I could get you to stop and think about what you were doing—about turning me in. I just needed to give you time. I know it's not your fault; it's all mine. But you were in shock, and you were making bad decisions. You wanted me to go without you, and I just couldn't do that. You always say that people make bad decisions when they're frustrated. That's what you were doing—making a bad decision because you were frustrated. I just needed to give you some time to get over the frustration so that you can make good decisions again. Good decisions—like sticking with me and moving to the Mexican Riviera."

Craig looked around at the room and at Zeke's wild face. *What should I do? Play along with him? Get serious with him? Try sex? I can't make a mistake. Stay silent, at least for now.*

"I knew that you'd want to be with me if you could. I just needed time to think of a way for that to happen—and I have thought of it. So don't worry, Craig. I have it all planned out."

"What plan?" Craig asked.

"I watched the news this morning. They reported from the Kearney home in Hibbing. I was pronouncing it wrong in my head. Did you know that it's 'car-nee'? The dad's name was Dan Kearney. His wife must have found a way to call for help not too long after we left. Maybe she just screamed a lot or something. They said it was a cold-blooded killing from a robbery. I always thought that cold-blooded meant there was lots of violence and blood. This wasn't violent or bloody, but that's what they called it. But they said that police are asking the community for any information—there is a tip line. So I don't think they have anything, at least not yet. I think we have time."

"Time for what?" Craig asked.

"For us to get away. Yeah, I think we have time. But probably not a lot of time. The longer we stay here, the greater the chance that we'll get tracked down somehow. I figure we have three nights, and then we need to get out of Duluth. So this is what I have planned. I went online and got into my dad's cloud drive. I used to work at the church sometimes, and he never changed the password.

"I downloaded the church's register. So I have a list of all the church members and who they live with. I also know how much they give to the collection basket. My plan is to spend three nights hitting the ones who are single. I can't take a chance on anyone who might have someone else in the house. You won't be with me, and I can't look after two or more people on my own. So I'm going to hit the single homes. I'll focus on people who are older—they probably have more cash around. We're after cash and nothing else, just like you've always said.

"I'm going to get in and get out. Three nights. Then we'll have enough cash to make a run for the Mexican border. We can make our way to South America. We can live there, Craig, you and me. We'll have to get jobs, and it might be real hard at first. But we'll be together in the sun. We can go running without our shirts on and have a great time."

Craig continued to look at Zeke's wild face. *He is an idiot, a complete lunatic. He knows nothing about borders or passports or working in foreign countries. There is no way we can drive all the way to Mexico without being tracked. And even if we could, I don't want to. I want this to end. This is not who I am. I am not a killer. I need this to end and for us both to go to jail—him a lot longer than me.*

"Craig?" Zeke asked. "What are you thinking? Is it a good plan?"

What am I thinking? That you're a completely insane lunatic. Three nights? You'll be caught for sure. You'll be—well, at least you won't be here, and I might be able to get away. You aren't smart enough to pull this off. You'll hit a house with a security system and get caught. I might be able to get out of this free and clear. Then Craig considered, *He might also take me along if I can convince him. Then I can take him down and run to the police.*

"Honestly," said Craig, "I think that your plan isn't half bad. But it would be better if there were two of us on each job. You'll never do it alone—too many things can go wrong. Let me go, and I can help you. We'll get the cash quicker, maybe in just one or two nights. Then we'll head to Mexico."

"I get what you're saying," Zeke replied. "But I can't trust you right now. You were going to turn me in, and I can't forget that. But I think that when I have the cash and I can keep an eye on you in the car, you'll start to remember what it feels like to be with me. You won't be frustrated anymore, and you'll be back to making good decisions. See, I have this theory that you are still in shock about me killing someone, and you can't really see me in the same way. But when we spend time together in the car, you'll remember who I am and what it feels like to be in love. So you should just stay right here and let me take care of things."

"But," said Craig, "I'm thirsty, and I'm going to get hungry. I have to go to the bathroom."

"There's a bucket right there for the bathroom. Sorry that it has to be like that. But I promise that I'll be good at emptying it and cleaning it. Just try not to be embarrassed. I'll get you some water, and I'll make sure you have plenty to eat before I go out tonight."

"What about Geno's? I'm supposed to work tomorrow."

"I sent an email to Karen from your account. I said—I mean, you said—that we're really sick. She knows that we live together. She won't want us to come in if we're both sick."

Should I ask for my phone? No, he'd never fall for that. I just need him to get out of here so that I can try to get out. Christ, I'm cold down here.

"Can I have a blanket?" Craig asked. "It's really cold down here."

"Of course. I just wanted to feel you."

29

CHECKS AND BALANCES

Zeke wanted to show Craig that he really loved him. He remembered his grandmother often saying that a way to a man's heart was through his stomach. He called a steakhouse and had them deliver a filet cooked medium-well with a side of broccoli. *Craig will be really glad that I went with the broccoli instead of the steak fries.* Zeke prepared a tray with a cloth napkin and Craig's food displayed on his best dishes. He took the tray down the stairs and set it on the mattress.

"I really wish I could stay and eat with you," Zeke said. "But I need to get started. It's already dark, and these old people tend to go to bed early."

Zeke bent over and gave Craig a kiss on the mouth. *I think he might have enjoyed that. He seemed to. I knew that love would get us through.* Zeke smiled at Craig, then turned and walked back up the stairs.

He had already packed the supply satchel, which was lying on the kitchen table. Zeke had hidden Craig's phone on the top of the refrigerator. He put his own phone next to it and grabbed the satchel from the table. He noticed a half-eaten bag of potato chips and a half-eaten chocolate cream pie on the counter. *Craig wouldn't like to see that. He'd hate me eating that stuff and would really hate the mess on the counter. But he won't see it. I'll make sure to clean it up before we leave for Mexico. I won't eat badly when we're together. He wants my body in top shape.*

On the kitchen table, Zeke left the register of his father's congregation. He'd memorized his targets earlier and didn't want to risk losing the papers along the way. He checked to make sure that all the doors were locked. He left the house, got into his car, and drove down the street.

The first house was that of Mrs. Edy McCabe.

After countless attempts, Craig had pretty much given up trying to escape from the handcuffs. *Of course, I had to buy the very best handcuffs I could find.* He had begun to contemplate the possibility of cutting his hand off. But he didn't have access to any tools that could do the job. *He didn't bring me a knife to use with the steak, even though he made an effort to use the good plates. He's being careful. I need to eat the broccoli. It will be good for me.*

I should have kicked him out of the car and called the cops back in Hibbing—the second he told me that he'd killed someone. That would have been the best for me. I should have turned us both in on the spot. I was being nice and wanted him to have a chance to escape. Stupid! People always take advantage of people who are nice. I learned that lesson long ago. How many times at the restaurant have I given a server the benefit of the doubt, and it's always come back to bite me in the ass?

He lay back on the mattress and wrapped the blanket around himself as best he could. Basements in Minnesota were cold even during the hottest months of the year. Duluth never had a really hot month. *I don't know why I'm freaking out over this. It's not like it's the first time I've been tied up.*

After he found his father dead on the couch, Craig had been made a ward of the state and put into the foster care program. He had no grandparents, and no other relatives had stepped forward to raise him either. Foster care had been a series of nightmares with an occasional dream thrown in once in a while, just to make the nightmares seem worse.

What was the name of that family with the older kids who were the worst to me? I can't remember their name at all. They lived by that old gas station. I wonder if the house is still there. There were four older kids—teenagers, all of them. The parents had no control. I was small, and they would tie me up and leave me that way all night. They didn't hurt me or anything, just tied me up. I think they were afraid I'd walk around the house and find out whatever it was they were doing that they didn't want me to see. Maybe the parents knew about it and also wanted me to stay put? I've never thought of that before.

For the first time since waking up from being drugged, Craig was tired. But it was impossible to sleep. *I'm going to have to be a lot more tired before I can sleep. It's too uncomfortable. What the hell is Zeke doing right now? I hope he gets caught soon. He's bound to make a lot of mistakes. What am I saying? Christ, he's not going to make any mistakes—he was a really good student. Will he tell the cops about me if he gets caught? Probably not. He'll want to protect me. I have to get out of here on my own.*

Craig inspected the handcuffs once again. His house was older, with heavy metal pipes. There was no slack in the handcuffs, the pipe, or his wrist. *If only someone would come to the door. I might hear them, and I could yell. Who am I kidding? Nobody is ever going to come to the door—I've worked hard at getting a life where I'm never bothered.*

30

ZEKE'S BIG NIGHT OUT

At 3:41 a.m., Zeke pulled back into Craig's driveway. Now that he was home, he felt comfortable enough to take off his black face mask. It had blood on it. *Shoot, I'm going to have to wash all this stuff. I better not let Craig see it. He'll know that I made some mistakes. But they weren't really mistakes, were they? I'm not sure what happens to me. Yes, I am. I'm doing what I can to get a really good life with Craig.*

Zeke grabbed the satchel and a larger plastic bag from the back seat. He got out of the car, quietly closed the door, and slowly walked toward the house. He used his key to open the side door.

He walked immediately to the bathroom and turned on the light. *Shoot, there is more blood than I thought.* He put the satchel and the bag in the bathtub and got to work cleaning himself up. He took a shower. *I have to be as clean as possible for Craig.* He left the satchel in the tub and carried the plastic bag with him to his bedroom. There, he put on just a pair of jeans—no underwear, shirt, or even socks. He went to the stairs. *I left the light on down there. I hope it didn't get in the way of him sleeping.*

When Zeke reached the bottom of the basement stairs, Craig was awake and staring at him. When Zeke saw this, he immediately ran over to Craig and started emptying the plastic bag full of cash on top of him. "Hey!" Zeke yelled. "Look at all this! I think it's over ten thousand! Boom! I knew we could do it."

"Okay," Craig replied calmly, "but you need to tell me exactly what happened."

"Aren't you happy? I thought you'd be really happy. This is a really good start. Two more nights of this, and we will have plenty of money to make it to Mexico. We still have the seven thousand I took from my dad and the money we've taken over the past year, which is another fourteen. That's over thirty thousand, and I still have two more nights."

"Yes," Craig replied, again in a robotic voice, "it's all very good. You did a great job. But tell me exactly what happened so that I can tell if you made any, uh, if you made me really proud of you. Which you did. Don't leave out anything."

Well, I can't tell him everything. He won't like that I shot someone. Leave out any mention of the gun and blood. "Okay, so I decided to start with Edy McCabe. I sort of remembered my dad talking about her, but I didn't really know her. She's a widow, the register said she's eighty-four, and she gives a one-hundred-dollar bill in her church envelope each week."

"Where does she live?"

"Over on Kenwood. Small, sort of old house. Don't worry, I wore all the blacks and a new pair of shoes. She'd left the living room window open. You were right—living in Duluth has an advantage for thieves during the summer because nobody has air conditioning. So I cut the screen with the knife—don't worry, I had on gloves, and I made sure that I had everything back in the satchel before I left. So I cut the screen with the knife and climbed in. It was dark, but I ended up on the couch.

"The LED headbands are probably the best things we've bought. I found the bedroom; it was just next to the living room on the main floor. I scared the crap out of her, of course. It took some time to get her to stop wailing. I held the gun on her, and she eventually got up and showed me a safe in her closet. It was one of those small units you can get at a regular store. She opened it, after several tries because she was nervous, and gave me a plastic bank zipper. She'd written $5,000 on the outside with marker. I checked it out—looked like about that much. I remembered what you said about how getting out quick is better than staying and haggling, especially if you get a lot. So I zip-tied one of her wrists to the bedpost. In the living room, I took the cash out and left the zipper bank bag on the floor—I remembered what you said about not taking extra stuff. Then I crawled out the window and ran to the car."

"You didn't take anything else? You weren't tempted to linger and look around?" Craig asked.

"Nope," Zeke replied, "not a bit. I was in and out with five grand. So the next house I picked was another widow. I think she plays the keyboard or something. But when I got there, no windows were open. So I used the universal pick on the back door. The lock was kind of crappy, but there was a security system that went off. So I locked the door and ran. I remembered what you said—people get security systems to keep you out, not to make sure you get caught. I got away, and who knows what happened. Maybe she just turned it off and went to bed, but if the cops came, they probably didn't notice anything.

"Next was Hank Neilson. Never married, age seventy-four. Worked in iron ore mining—some sort of big shot. That's actually what my dad wrote in the register, that he was a big shot. He gave a ten-thousand-dollar check to the church every Christmas. Now, he's got a nice big rambler up on Arrowhead, a newer home. Only one window was open, and I could hear a fan just inside the window. I was very careful and cut the screen. I was being careful not to hit the fan, but then I noticed that I had crawled right into the bedroom—he was sleeping just a few feet from me!

"I turned on the light. Now this guy was a real piece of work. He started swearing like you wouldn't believe—using the f-bomb and everything. You'd think he was in charge! When he calmed down, he acted really huffy and went to his wallet. He had, like, less than two hundred in there. I haggled for a bit, then remembered what you said and got out." *I think he believed that,* Zeke thought. *Good.* "Then," Zeke continued, "I went—"

"Wait a second," Craig interrupted. "Did you look around the iron ore man's house for any other signs of cash?"

"Yeah, for just a moment, but I didn't want to waste time." *He's suspicious. He'll freak out if I tell him that I shot the guy in the head.* "Remember," said Zeke, "the longer you stay, the more of a chance that you'll make a mistake."

"Yes, I remember," Craig replied. "I taught you that."

"And you are a great teacher." *Go on—don't talk about all the blood and the carpet. Just tell him about the last one. It's really cold down here. I should have put on a shirt and some socks.* "So just one more," Zeke continued. "Sarah Dockindorf. She's forty-six—you know, one of those women who never got married. She's a nurse, which is amazing because her house reeked of smoke—seriously, you would have been sick. She has an old home in one of those hillside neighborhoods outside of downtown, a real dump. But she's given a lot to the church, so I thought I'd take a chance on it. Real easy to get inside—she left the inside door open, with just the screen door shut. It was locked, but how hard is it to cut a screen and unlock the door? She can't be too bright. She can't make a very good nurse.

"Anyway, I step into the kitchen. I've got the headlamp on. There's crap all over the place—you know, like you see on television, a real hoarder. And it stinks so bad of smoke and God knows what. There was probably a dead cat somewhere in there, for sure. There's pots and pans on all the cupboards. Junk everywhere. The next room was some sort of office. The only place that didn't have a pile of stuff on it was a desk in the corner. I figure that she must actually sit there sometimes. So I started to go through the desk and found a drawer full of cash. I tried to count it as I loaded the satchel but stopped when I reached five grand. I could get in and out of this place without any notice at all. That was good because I was still covered in blood and thought it best to get away. So I just left and—"

"You were covered in what?" Craig interrupted. "Blood?"

Shit! You're so stupid! You're so stupid! Play it low. Make up some-thing small. "Oh yeah," Zeke replied, "I forgot to mention that I cut my hand with the knife. But I was really, really careful to not get blood on anything. It was just a little blood anyway."

"But you said you were still covered in blood. Covered in blood is not just a little blood. What happened?"

"Nothing. I swear. I cut my hand when I was using the knife to cut the screen."

"Show me your hand."

"God, Craig! I thought you trusted me more. I'm not showing you my hand. You should be so happy right now. We are going to be able to get away and live together. I'm putting myself out there so that we can be happy."

Zeke began grabbing all the cash and stuffing it back into the plastic bag. Craig didn't stop him. *What the hell is wrong with him? Maybe he's just looking out for me—that's what he's doing. He wants to make sure I didn't make a mistake, or that if I did make a mistake, he can try to fix it. He's not ever going to turn me in, not now that he has all this money. I need to be nicer to him.*

"It's okay," Zeke said when he'd finished collecting the cash. "I'm sorry that I got mad at you. I know that you're just looking out for our best interest. I'm going to put this away. Then I'll come back and clean your bathroom bucket. Then we can get some sleep—I'm tired. Make room for me. I'll be back."

I need to wash all those bloody clothes. He'll hear me and wonder about it. I need an excuse to use the washing machine at this hour. "I'm going to wash that blanket—it smells," Zeke said, grabbing the blanket from around Craig. "I'll bring you another one while it's in the washing machine." *He's looking at me suspiciously. What he doesn't know won't hurt him. God, he looks so hot lying there like that, with his abs and chest exposed. He's going to get cold.*

31

THE CANDLESTICK

Craig slept for several hours. For most of that time, Zeke slept next to him. Pangs of hunger grew intense inside of Zeke. *I'm glad Craig has slept so long. He needed it. But I'll have to wake him up to get out of bed. I have to get something to eat. He's probably hungry too.* Zeke rolled to the edge of the mattress and stood up on the concrete floor of the basement. The floor was very cold, and he was wearing only boxer shorts. He pranced over to the stairs, attempting to touch the concrete as little as possible.

It took him about an hour to dress and drive to Bulldog Pizza for a large pepperoni. Bulldog Pizza, named for the local college's sports teams, had been his favorite for as long as he could remember. Zeke also stopped at the nearby grocery store to buy parmesan cheese. *Craig loves parmesan cheese—at least when he allows himself to eat poorly.* When Zeke returned home, he rummaged through the cupboards, looking for a glass container that would elegantly display the parmesan on the tray with the pizza. *I'm not just going to put a plastic green container on the tray. He deserves more than that. I should have taken a parmesan shaker from Geno's the last time I was there. I wonder how they're doing up there at the restaurant. They probably miss both of us a lot.*

He found an appropriate container in the cabinet where Craig stored his nicer kitchen items. Then something in the back caught his eye: a pair of large brass candlesticks. *Craig's got some nice stuff around here. I guess when you're in your forties, you've had some time to get nice stuff to use when company comes over.* Zeke grabbed one of the candlesticks. It was heavy. He set the parmesan container on the kitchen table and used the candlestick as a sword, slashing it through the air.

Like all kids growing up in Duluth, Zeke had been raised on the tale of Minnesota's most famous homicides. Zeke thought about the case as he sliced the air with the heavy brass instrument. *I did a report on Glensheen—I think I must have been in seventh grade, maybe? I was fascinated with it. Maybe it was sixth grade? I can't remember the teacher's name, but I think I remember that I liked her.*

Glensheen was an enormous estate on the shore of Lake Superior in Duluth. The house itself was 20,000 square feet. It had been built in 1908 by the richest family in Minnesota, the Congdons. In 1977, only the Congdons' youngest daughter was still living at Glensheen. Elizabeth Congdon was eighty-three years old and in poor health. She lived alone but was cared for, around the clock, by a rotating group of private nurses. Elizabeth was extremely wealthy.

On a dark June night, someone broke into Glensheen through a window. Zeke thought he remembered that it was a window in the basement. The intruder headed up toward the bedrooms. But on the grand staircase, the person ran into the night nurse who was taking care of the old woman. He grabbed a candlestick and beat the nurse with it until she was dead. Then he went up and smothered the old woman with a pillow until she was dead. The authorities never determined who had done it for sure, but everyone knew it had been the old woman's daughter and the daughter's husband. They had both gone on trial, if Zeke remembered right. *I think the daughter got off, but the husband got sent to prison for just a couple of years and was let go on a technicality. I can't remember exactly why. Pizza's getting cold. I must have driven past that mansion a thousand times. Every time, I think of the murders. I suppose most kids in Duluth do.*

Zeke put the candlestick in the satchel and took the dinner to Craig.

"I'm going to turn the light off this time," said Zeke as he walked up the stairs with the dinner tray. "I'll be back in a few hours, I guess. We'll be more than halfway done after tonight, Craig. It won't be long now, and you'll be able to get off that bed. You should start thinking about what you want to bring to Mexico, but it will probably be best to pack light. Just let me know tomorrow what you want, and I'll get your things together. I'll make sure that the car is full of gas for the first leg. Okay then, I'll see you later."

"Hey, Zeke," said Craig, attempting to sound as normal as possible, "do you think we could go for a run tomorrow? I mean, before you go out for the night. I really have to work out. My body is starting to go soft. You should probably get in some exercise too. It'd be good for both of us. We'll be going on a long car trip, and we'll need to run off some energy."

"Um ..." Zeke hesitated for several seconds. "I ... I just don't think so. Let's wait until we get to Mexico. I promise, Craig, that we'll have lots of time to work out together. I'd never let your body go bad. And I'm always going to stay in shape for you."

Christ, I thought he might fall for that. Craig watched as Zeke climbed the stairs. He could hear Zeke walking around upstairs, most likely changing clothes. Then, several minutes later, he heard the door close.

I have to get out of here. He's completely lost it. I know he killed someone last night, or at least hurt someone real bad, if he ended up covered in blood. Probably that Neilson guy who was supposed to have all that money and then didn't. Not getting money seems to be Zeke's trigger. He's probably got some kind of daddy complex too. I guess we all do.

By this time, Craig's wrist was raw from pulling on the handcuffs. *My wrist hurts. Everything hurts. I just don't have anything to use. This damn mattress is memory foam—I don't even have a metal spring I could rip out. I've looked around this basement a thousand times. I can't find anything. I wish all of this were different. I want to call the cops, turn in Zeke, and return the Sinclair Lewis urn—serve whatever time they give me and then start all over again. I own this house outright. I think I get to keep it while I'm in prison. But I might as well sell it and let the money earn interest while I'm locked up.*

Even the cup of water he left is plastic. He took everything else away. I could have broken the glass parmesan container and maybe used it, but he took it.

I always thought there was a chance I'd get caught stealing and go to prison for a few years. I was ready for that. I'd have said I was guilty and not even had a trial. But now I'm an accessory to murder. And I might end up dead myself if I can't get out of here. Either he'll kill me, or I'll die of starvation. What will I do if he never comes back and nobody comes for me? He might get shot in the middle of a burglary and die. Nobody will know to look for me. I don't think anyone will hear me yell from down here. I wonder how long the neighbors will tolerate the grass growing before they complain. Probably pretty long.

But what if he pulls it off? What if he gets through the third night? If he tries to take me to Mexico, I'll have a real chance to escape. It's a long drive, and he'll have to sleep. My best chance is probably to play along. Hopefully, he won't figure out that it's impossible to take me all the way to Mexico. I don't think he will. I always wanted to plan the perfect crime. I came near but still made mistakes. But there is one thing I was absolutely perfect at—making him fall completely in love with me. That will be either my triumph or my end. Christ, the stress is making me into a damn poet. That's not good. People who are lost in their thoughts make many mistakes.

32

ZEKE'S BIGGER NIGHT OUT

The sun had already begun its spectacular ascent over Lake Superior when Zeke finally pulled into the driveway. *I've been gone too long this time. He'll be worried.* He bent over and grabbed the bloody candlestick that was lying on the floor of the passenger side of the car. *I don't want to get blood in the satchel. I'll take this thing in the shower with me to wash it. But it's all bent out of shape. I'll probably have to wash it and then throw it in the lake or something. Wouldn't it be something if I could get rid of it at Glensheen? That's not a good idea, but it would be kind of cool.*

Zeke quietly stepped out of the car. He realized that he was still wearing his mask and quickly snatched it off his head. It was wet. *Guess I'll have to wash again. I've got a lot more blood on me than I did last night. Oh yeah, I wanted to watch the morning news to see about the reports. Or maybe I shouldn't. It might stop me if I hear they have clues. Should I ask Craig about it? No, idiot. He can't know all the details. I'll avoid the news. Just one more night.*

It took Zeke just under an hour to get everything cleaned up. He walked down the steps wearing only jeans again and turned on the light. Craig was awake.

"Hey," said Zeke. "Good morning, handsome." *I've never called him that before. It feels so good.*

"Back at ya," said Craig.

That feels good too. He seems happy. He's probably happy that we'll be out of here soon. The floor is cold. I should get Craig some socks before he gets off the mattress tomorrow. "I left the money upstairs this time so that I don't have to pick it all up like I did yesterday. But don't worry—there is a lot of it. In less than twenty-four hours, we can be on our way. We'll have plenty of everything. But I've been thinking. I don't think we'll stop at a grocery store in Duluth before we leave. Let's not chance it. I think we'll drive a few hours and then stop at a grocery store for things like water and snacks."

"Well, how did it all go tonight?" Craig asked. "Tell me everything."

Zeke walked over and sat down on the bed. Craig was covered with the blanket. *Damn. I want him so badly. I hate that blanket. But I don't want him to be uncomfortable if I rip it off.* "So first up was Lisa Sumner. She's forty-nine years old, a divorced attorney with no kids."

"Did your dad keep these notes on everyone?"

"Yep. He did it so that he could brush up on a person before they came into his office."

"That's actually pretty smart."

"I guess. Unless your notes fall into the wrong hands."

"Any news reports?" Craig asked. "Anybody making the connection that all the victims are from the same church?"

Should I tell him that I've been avoiding the news? No, I'll keep him relaxed. But now I do wonder if anyone has realized that the houses all belong to people from the same church. I bet Mom and Dad have. I wonder if they'd dare say anything. I'll just make something up for Craig. "They are reporting that there have been robberies. But they say there are no leads. They haven't said anything about the church. I think we'll be okay. Just remember, it's just a few more hours."

Get back to it, Zeke told himself. "So like I said, Lisa Sumner is divorced. She lives up by the Catholic college. But here's the good news—she wasn't home. I got in by picking the back door. It was easy. I looked all around, saw all the bedrooms, but there was nobody in the house. I have to say—it was kind of nice to have the place to myself, like I could take some time to look around. But like you always told me, I didn't want to get distracted or caught up in the moment. Get in and get out.

"I had to go through desk drawers and closets—couldn't find anything. I even checked under the mattress. I couldn't turn on any of the lights because I was afraid that the neighbors might know she wasn't home. But then I found an envelope in the same drawer as her bras. It had exactly eighteen hundred dollars in it. I took the cash, left the envelope, and got out of there immediately. I think you'd be proud of the way I resisted temptation and didn't take anything else—even jewelry. It would have been easy to take a bunch of stuff that was all right there, but I didn't."

"I am very proud of you," Craig said.

God, that makes me feel good, like a special feeling in my stomach. "Just wait—the best is coming up," Zeke said. "The second house, some old woman named Thompson, was out by the mall, but still a Duluth address. But when I got there, something was just not quite right. It's hard to explain, but there was a light on in the garage—not in the house, just the garage. It just didn't feel right, so I ran back to the car and aborted that target."

"Wise choice," said Craig. "Trust your instincts."

"Thanks. But the third house was the big hit of the night—Charles Hendricks, but Dad wrote that he is called Chucky. I don't know why anyone would want to be called Chucky. He's a cook at a school somewhere—single, never married. A real crappy, small house in West Duluth. Seriously, a real crap-hole. The door was unlocked. I found the bedroom really fast, but the door was closed. I could hear a really loud fan through the door. So I decided to try and see what I could find. But don't worry—I was very careful to make sure that I was always alert with one eye on the bedroom door, just in case he came out. I had the gun ready.

"Of course, I was ready to wake him up if I didn't find anything outside the bedroom. But then I found the big stash. He had a pile of books about wildlife art on top of a small cabinet. Inside the cabinet was a plastic tub, one of those shoe-box-size tubs. It was full of cash—like, a lot of cash, Craig. I didn't want to make noise, so I just took the whole plastic box. I know that I shouldn't have taken it and should have just left with the cash, but I didn't really have a choice. I wanted to get out while he was still sleeping."

"That was probably a smart thing to do," said Craig. "Besides, there are tons of those small plastic tubs out there. It will be really hard to track down."

"That's what I thought too! I just left and ran back to the car. I drove down to Canal Park and counted the money in the car. That's what took me so long. Get this, handsome—fifteen thousand in large bills!"

"Wow, that's amazing!"

"I know! I was stoked! So we have almost fifty thousand at this point. But I'm not done. The last house was on the Point, past the lift bridge. I knew it was getting to be almost early morning, but I was so close to it. So I went to Anna Carlson, age seventy-two, a widow. Gives twenty bucks each week to the church, but I thought I'd give it a chance. The house was right on the lake. Pretty nice. A window was open, so I split the screen and crawled in. I woke her up. She was scared but gave me nine hundred dollars, and I left. So that's it—a pretty good night."

"Wait. You rushed the end. The house on the Point—did you tie her up? You left out some details."

I left out a lot of details on that one. There wasn't any need to tie her up. "Yeah, I tied her up. Used the zip ties. I got the money and left—just like you said." *I think he probably bought that. Quit while you're ahead and finish cleaning up.* "So I'm going to clean out your bucket and get ready for bed. I'll be back in a few minutes. I know it's already morning, but we can get in a couple of hours of sleep at least. There won't be any sleep for me after that since I have a busy night, and then we need to get on the road. I'll get some energy drinks from the gas station when I fill up. But aren't you proud of me?"

"I'm very proud of you, Zeke. We have plenty—you don't even need to do a third night. Let's just head out right now."

"I thought about that, but then I thought that this is our last chance. We'll never have time on our side again. So we're going to go ahead with it all. Trust my instincts, like you said. I'll be back in a few minutes."

Zeke got up, took the bucket from the floor, and headed toward the stairs. "Oh yeah," said Zeke, pausing on the steps, "I'm going to wash some stuff. Nothing from tonight, but some stuff I need to pack for Mexico. So if you hear the washing machine, that's why."

33

MEANWHILE AT THE RESTAURANT

A young woman walked into Geno's Restaurant near the Miller Hill Mall in Duluth. It had been a long day, and it was past her dinnertime. She was starving. She requested a table in the corner of the dining room. She wanted some quiet after several hectic hours.

"What's the best pasta on the menu?" she asked the server who approached her.

"Do you like Alfredo sauce?" the server replied.

"Yeah—love it."

"Then get the fettuccini. It's fantastic."

"Fine. Bring me that and an iced tea with lemon, if you have one."

"No worries."

It took just a minute for the server to return with the tea. The woman poured in a packet of pink sweetener from a small container on the table.

"Just one more thing," the young woman said. "Is there a manager around I can talk to?"

The server, a bit surprised by the question, said, "Not right now. We are a manager short. But the owner is here."

"Yes, that would be great. Can you send zir out here?"

"Zir?" the server questioned.

"It's what you say when you don't know someone's gender. I don't know if the owner is a her or him, so I used zir."

"Okay, I …well, I guess that's cool. Just a second. I'll get her—I mean, it's a female lady."

The young woman sat back in her chair and rolled her head around on her shoulders, relaxing her neck. She quickly drank almost all of her tea. After a few minutes, an older woman with red hair came out of the kitchen and approached her.

"Hello, I'm Karen O'Neil. I'm the owner of Geno's. The server said that you wanted to talk to me?"

"Yes, thank you for coming over. My name is Shaynah Williams. I work for the Minnesota Bureau of Criminal Apprehension." She gave Karen one of her cards. "Do you have a few minutes? Could you sit here for a bit?"

Karen looked at the card, checked to see that there weren't any other customers near the table, and sat down. "What can I do for you?" Karen asked hesitantly.

"I'm in Duluth investigating a number of credit card fraud cases. You're probably not aware of this, but nine different people who have had their credit card numbers stolen during the last year dined at this restaurant. I'm investigating because it's a bit too much of a coincidence. Can you think of anything you've seen or heard that might indicate your restaurant has a problem in this area?"

"Well," said Karen, a bit defensively, "of course I've not seen or heard anything. This is the first I've heard that such a thing might be happening. You said that it's been going on for a year?"

"At least that long. It's taken us a long time to track it down."

"I have great employees here. Is there any other proof that it's Geno's? I mean, people use their cards at a lot of places."

"I'm not doubting that you have great employees. And really, you aren't in any trouble at this point. But it might be helpful if I could get a tour of your restaurant. It would be great to see where the servers charge the cards and where other people might have access to the information."

The server approached with Shaynah's fettuccini and another iced tea.

"Thank you," said Shaynah. "This looks fantastic."

"It is fantastic," said Karen. "Even if I say so myself. And this is on the house."

"No, really, I can't accept that."

"It's not a problem," said Karen.

"Yes, it is. It's illegal," Shaynah replied.

"Oh—right. I'm really sorry. I just didn't think. I'm used to doing business with businesspeople. I didn't really think. But of course, I will show you our procedures. You can see anything you want. I'll let you finish your pasta, and then we can have a tour."

"That would be great. I'm starving, and this is really good."

Karen got up from the table.

Between mouthfuls, Shaynah said, "Oh, and also, does anyone work here who is a male—a white male—in his mid-thirties to mid-forties, athletic, sort of good-looking? Dark hair with a trimmed dark beard?"

"Well," Karen replied, again hesitantly, "we have one person who fits that description. He's one of the managers here. But he's been out ill for the last few days. Why? Is he a suspect? Do you think he took people's credit card numbers? I really can't believe that. He's been a very good manager for a really long time. Everyone loves him here."

"Maybe," Shaynah replied, "but I really can't say anything about that right now. Can you get me his name and contact information?"

"Sure, I guess that would be all right, since you gave me your card. His name is Craig Kellerman. I'll get you his number and address from the back."

"Oh, and he doesn't use a wheelchair, does he?"

"No," Karen replied. "In fact, he's quite a runner. Very athletic. He doesn't need a wheelchair."

"I didn't think so," Shaynah said.

34

GRANDMA'S APRON

Zeke got on his tiptoes to grab Craig's vibrating phone from the top of the refrigerator. *I don't recognize that number, and Craig obviously doesn't have it saved in his contacts. It's probably a robocall. God, how many times are they going to call?*

The sun had begun to drop behind the hillside of Duluth, and though it was still light outside, Zeke turned on the kitchen light so that he could see better. A timer went off over the oven. Zeke turned off the timer, put on one oven mitt, opened the oven, and retrieved a single tray of freshly baked cookies. *These smell great! He is going to freak that we are having cookies for dinner. But I know that he's going to insist on eating healthy once we leave tomorrow, so this is our last chance to eat something like cookies. He'll understand. I don't want to go out to get dinner.*

Zeke was barefoot and wore only jeans and his grandma's apron—the apron he'd taken from his parents' house when he robbed them. *I guess this damn apron is the only trophy I've taken from a job. Figures. I wonder what Mom would think about me wearing it to bake cookies for my hot gay husband. This apron used to hurt like hell when she'd snap at my bare butt with it. Now I get to wear it in love for my husband. Mom can go screw herself—but she probably doesn't know how.*

He used a plastic spatula to place the cookies on a nice plate. Craig's phone vibrated again on top of the refrigerator. *Ignore it. We should probably destroy our phones when we leave for Mexico—throw them in the lake.* He picked up the plate of cookies and headed downstairs. Craig was sleeping.

"Hey, handsome," Zeke said as he crossed the floor. "Sorry to wake you."

Craig opened his eyes, took a moment, and then sat up on the mattress. He leaned against the concrete block wall and the sewer pipe that he was attached to.

"Now don't get all preachy on me. I know—I know that cookies are really bad. But it's our last night in this house, and I didn't want to go out to get dinner. This house has been really special for me. I want to cherish it, sort of. So are cookies okay?"

"They're fine, Zeke. No need to worry," Craig replied. "It's actually kind of touching."

I knew he'd understand. He's the best. Zeke set the plate on the floor and grabbed the blanket that was covering Craig. He jerked it off and threw it across the room. "I want to watch you eat cookies—I mean really watch your muscles as you eat. Is that weird?"

"Yes," said Craig, "but I don't mind. You should lose that apron, though. It's creepy, and then I can see your muscles too."

So freaking hot! Zeke took off the apron and flung it on the floor.

"You've really changed a lot this year," Craig said. "I mean, your body has changed a lot. You are way more muscular than when you moved in here. And you're even more different than when you first started working at the restaurant."

"I was just a kid then. You made me into a man." *I can't wait.* Zeke bent over the mattress and kissed Craig on the lips, long and hard. *It's been too many days since we've had sex. I can't wait.* He threw himself on top of Craig. *Oh God, this feels so good.*

They made out for a few minutes. Zeke started to feel Craig all over. Then he noticed that Craig was not responding as he normally did. Zeke kept at it for several more minutes but then stopped when Craig still had not shown an anatomical reaction.

"Everything okay?" Zeke asked. "You seem into it up here, but not really down there."

"Of course, I'm into it. I just can't get comfortable with the handcuffs. Can't you take them off? I want to feel you all over. You look hot in those jeans—I've been thinking about that every time you come down here. But I didn't know you wanted to get into it until now. You can put them back on as soon as we're done—the handcuffs, I mean. Your jeans you can keep off as long as you want."

"Yeah, that would be okay. I guess you can't get too far, at least while we're holding on to each other."

Craig laughed a bit.

It feels so good to hear him laugh, Zeke thought. *Mexico is going to be great.*

Zeke quickly ran up the stairs, leaving the plate of cookies on the floor. Just a moment later, he came bounding back down the stairs, skipping every other step, carrying a single key. Zeke lay on top of Craig. He unlocked the handcuffs and put both the cuffs and the key on the same plate as the cookies.

"Oh yes, that feels great," Craig said as he rubbed his wrist. "Thanks. I'm so much more comfortable now."

"I'm sorry that you had to be like this," said Zeke. "I really am. But I was right. You just needed time to get over your frustration so that you could make better choices. Now aren't you glad that you didn't turn me in? We have all this money and get to be together in Mexico."

"No more talking." Craig started to kiss Zeke passionately.

They began feeling each other all over. Zeke worked his hands down and, after a few minutes, noticed that Craig was still not responding. As soon as Zeke physically felt his unresponsiveness, Craig shoved him hard into the concrete block wall of the basement.

God! That hurt like hell! "What the hell are you thinking?" Zeke screamed.

But Craig was already up and off of the mattress. Zeke realized that Craig was trying to escape and pushed himself away from the wall. He pounced on the mattress and got a hold of Craig's right ankle. Craig fell to the floor, on top of the plate of cookies and handcuffs. Craig grabbed the handcuffs and threw them across the room.

"Stop!" Zeke yelled. "You're ruining everything!"

Craig turned, still on the floor, and pushed Zeke back to the mattress. He got up, but again, Zeke was able to pounce off the mattress and grab his leg.

"What are you doing?" Zeke asked loudly. "You're ruining everything! I love you. You love me, remember? We're going to Mexico, so just stop it! Get control of yourself."

"I don't love you!" Craig shouted back at the top of his voice. "I'm not even gay, you sick fuck!" Craig kicked hard and hit Zeke in the head.

Shit! That hurts!

Craig jumped off the floor and ran to the steps. But Zeke was fast—too fast for Craig. In an instant, he grabbed onto Craig's back. Craig fell against the stairs. He struggled to overturn Zeke, but Zeke was on top and had the upper hand. Zeke reached into his jeans pocket and took out a syringe. He fumbled with it a bit. *I'm so glad I've always kept one of these in my pocket.* Craig never saw the syringe. Zeke popped the cap off and stuck it into Craig's upper arm. He pushed the plunger. Craig yelled and continued to struggle. Zeke held on with all his strength until Craig finally relaxed and succumbed on the stairs.

Zeke stayed on top of him. *I used to love feeling him breathe up and down.* Zeke got up and pulled Craig's unconscious body down the stairs and across the floor. *That would hurt if he could feel it.* He threw Craig onto the mattress and went to find the handcuffs. But he saw the apron first.

Zeke's mind went blank, as it had before. He took the apron and twisted it tightly into a long rope. He went to the mattress and flipped Craig onto his stomach. He ripped Craig's boxers from his body. Zeke started whipping Craig with the apron, just as his mom had done to him.

Craig's back and buttocks grew red from the abuse, but the apron never broke his skin. Then Zeke got on top of Craig and wrapped the apron around his neck. He pulled as tight as he could. Craig began to convulse. The seizures lasted a long time—longer than they had for Dan Kearney. Finally, they stopped.

Zeke pulled away the apron and threw it by the plate of cookies that was still sitting on the floor. He turned Craig over on the mattress. Craig's eyes were halfway open. His lips were blue and slightly parted. *God, he looks so hot even now. What a body.*

Zeke got up, went upstairs, and changed into his black clothes. *One more night, and I'm out of here. Why did he have to ruin it all? It was so perfect.*

35

THEIR TASKS END

Shaynah Williams pulled into Craig Kellerman's driveway. The sky had just turned completely dark. She thought it was maybe too late to be doing this work, but she wanted to complete the task and head home to St. Paul.

She picked up a clipboard full of papers, stuffed her wallet in her pocket, and stepped out of the car. A light was on inside the house, shining out from a window on the side. Shaynah walked up to the front door and rang the doorbell. She waited. Everything seemed fairly normal as she looked around the front yard. She rang the bell again. Still, nobody came to the door. She sighed.

She decided to take a peek around the side and back of the house before heading back to her car. While proceeding past the window with the light on, she glanced inside and saw it was a kitchen. Then she saw something that completely captivated her attention. Right there, sitting on the kitchen table, was the urn that had once held Sinclair Lewis's ashes. It was now being used as a vase, with a bunch of dead flowers sticking out of it.

Shaynah knew the urn well. She'd studied the photograph of it so many times over the last year that it was etched perfectly in her memory. She grabbed her phone from her pocket and dialed a number.

"Hi," Shaynah said into the phone, "can I get Detective Anders?"

She looked long and hard at the urn while she waited on the phone. She really did not want to leave the house without it.

"Detective Anders," said a voice on the phone.

"Hi, yeah, this is Shaynah Williams from the BCA. I'm really sorry for bothering you again. I know that you are incredibly busy with all the stuff going on in Duluth right now."

"It's a crazy night, for sure," the detective said. "Everyone in Duluth is on edge."

"I hope you catch them tonight."

"I do too. I'm not sure the town can take another night. But we do have a pretty promising lead—there is a connection between all the victims."

"That's good."

"But how can I help you?" Detective Anders asked.

"I'm over at Craig Kellerman's house. This is the guy I talked to you about earlier—I sent you his info by text."

"Yep. And like I said, no record."

"Well, he has one now. I'm at his house right now. I tried calling his phone number a bunch of times, and he never answered. Nobody is home that I can see. However, I'm looking at one of the stolen items from a museum as we speak—the urn from Sauk Centre's Sinclair Lewis Center."

"Really? You're inside the house?"

"No, it's on the kitchen table, and the light is on. I can see it as clear as day. I know it's a lot to ask in the current circumstances, with your guys being really stretched tonight. But I really don't want to see the urn slip away. And there's a chance he's got the other items in there too."

"I can understand," Detective Anders said. "I imagine that a lot of people would like to see those things again. I'll tell you what—just hang on over there. I can be there in about ten or fifteen minutes. If it's in plain sight, then I can take some photos, and we might be able to get a search warrant, even on a night like this. But if he comes home, he'll be able to do whatever he wants until we get the warrant."

"Hey, I really appreciate your trying at least," Shaynah said. "It's been a long time coming, and it'd be good to have something concrete to report for once."

"Just hang tight. Be there soon."

Shaynah terminated the call and put the phone back in her pocket. Then she turned quickly as she heard someone walking up the driveway behind her.

After leaving the house for his final night of crime, Zeke turned into the park where he and Craig had often run together. He pulled into one of the spots outside the picnic shelter. There was nobody else around. *I want to get out and run like I used to with Craig. It would feel good to run. But I'll get eaten alive by mosquitos if I get out of the car right now.*

He turned off the car and just sat there. *What am I doing? It's over. He's gone, and nothing really matters anymore. I should just go to Mexico by myself and start over. I have plenty of money. Nobody will miss me here. Why'd you have to say those things, Craig? Why did you have to ruin it all?*

The cops have to know that all the victims went to the same church by now. I'm sure they've talked to Dad about it. He won't tell them about me. There's no way he's going to say his son might be a murderer—and there's especially no way he's going to say that his son is living with another man, if he even knows that. Even if there are lives on the line, he'll not say anything about having a gay son. I know him.

But why chance it? Why risk another night? I've got plenty of money. If I were a cop, I'd have every older church person who lives alone under surveillance. I should just cut my losses and move on. It just doesn't feel right to continue.

Craig, I really wanted to go to Mexico with you. I know you were running from me because you thought I was a killer. But I'm not. I was doing it all for you. As soon as we got safely away, I was going to go back to being me. We could have been so happy. But now there is nothing—except that I can start again, in Mexico. I can tell people that I just lost the great love of my life—people eat that stuff up. I'll find someone else to care about me.

Craig turned on the ignition and backed out of the parking spot. *I feel so relieved that I've made this decision. I just need an hour or so at home, and then I'll be on my way. Interstate 35 begins in Duluth and heads all the way to the border—just one road.*

He turned out of the park and drove toward home. On the way, he passed the enormous Glensheen estate, a high black iron fence encircling it. Like always, he thought about the killings that had occurred in there. *The candlestick on the stairs killed the nurse. She was beaten to death, just like that little kid last night. Craig was worth it.*

Zeke drove for a few more minutes and then turned down Craig's street. He was nearly at the house when he noticed a strange car parked in the driveway. He was shocked to see a woman standing by the kitchen window. *She's looking in and talking on the phone. Who the hell is she? She's not in a uniform. Might still be a cop. But why is she here? God, this could be really bad.*

He immediately pulled over on the side of the road. He put the satchel around his torso but held the gun in his hand. He got out of the car as quietly as he could. He walked in her direction.

36

ZEKE'S BIG NIGHT IN

Zeke walked up the driveway and headed directly toward the woman. She turned suddenly and faced him.

"Who are you?" Zeke asked with no emotion. He kept his hand holding the gun in his pocket. He kept his other hand in the other pocket because he was wearing black gloves, and he didn't want her to see them.

"Oh, hi," she replied. "Are you—no, you're too young to be Craig Kellerman. Do you live here?"

"Who are you?" Zeke repeated.

"My name is Shaynah Williams. I work for the Minnesota Bureau of Criminal Apprehension." She took a business card from her clipboard and held it out to him. He didn't take it.

"Are you a cop?"

"No, I'm a field forensic specialist. I'm an investigator. But I'm looking for Craig Kellerman. Do you know him?"

Zeke just stood there and stared at her. *What is she doing here? She doesn't look too alarmed if she thinks I'm the killer. And if she's not a cop, then what is she? If she knew I was the guy killing people in Duluth, I'd already have been taken down.*

"Are you okay?" Shaynah asked him. "You don't look too good."

"I'm fine," he said.

"Look, I'm waiting for the Duluth police. They'll be here any minute. I just got off the phone with them. I think it would be a good idea for you to stay right there, and I will stay right here, until they come."

The police are coming. They'll find him. They'll find me before I can get to Mexico. She's going—wait. This is the way. Craig is giving me my freedom, again. He does love me. I knew it. He's telling me exactly what to do. Zeke pulled a small ring with one key on it from his left pants pocket. He threw it at Shaynah's feet. She jumped a little.

"Take that key and open the side door," he instructed.

"No, I'm not doing that. We're just going to stay right where we are until the police get here."

Zeke took the gun out from his other pocket. She gasped and jumped backward when she saw it.

"Listen, I've killed a lot of people in the last week. So if you want to stay alive, then pick up that key and open the back door." *Look at her eyes. I completely surprised her. She's in shock and terrified. She's some kind of investigator—perfect. She doesn't have a weapon, or she'd have shown it already.*

Shaynah bent over slowly and picked up the key. She looked back at Zeke, and he used the gun to motion toward the side door. He followed her toward it. It was intensely dark around the door. Zeke was still wearing his black clothes, but his mask and LED light were in the satchel. After fumbling around for a few seconds, Shaynah was able to unlock the door. The light from the kitchen spilled outside.

"Now go inside. I'll follow you."

She did as she was told. Zeke stepped in after her.

Leave the door wide open. Leave it open for the cops. I need the cops to catch me this time. "Okay, go through the kitchen. Turn right. Now down the hall. Now open that door and head down the stairs."

Shaynah opened the door and started walking down the steps. As soon as she got halfway down the stairs, Zeke flipped on the basement light. It took her a moment to comprehend what she was seeing.

Then she screamed. Zeke used the gun to push her all the way down the stairs and into the middle of the room.

"Is that Craig Kellerman?" she asked harshly. "Is he dead?"

"Yes and yes." *He's also naked. You didn't comment on that.*

"Listen," Shaynah said as she turned toward him, "just let me go. I promise I won't say anything. I'm just a forensic scientist, really. I'm not a cop. I'll—"

"Just stop talking," Zeke interrupted. "We're going to wait right here. It won't be long now."

"I can take you to the Twin Cities if you want—or even farther. Wherever you want to go. I'll give you as much time as you need."

Just then, Zeke heard the sound of a car pulling into the drive, followed by the slam of a door. They stood in silence in the basement.

"Ms. Williams?" a voice yelled from somewhere upstairs. "You in there? It's Detective Anders. Is everything okay?"

"Tell him that you're not okay," said Zeke. "Tell him that you need help."

"I need help!" Shaynah yelled. "I'm in the basement."

"I have backup," said the voice, now quite loudly. "We're coming in. This the police—we are inside your home."

Zeke heard footsteps above.

"Craig, no!" Zeke shouted at the top of his lungs, making Shaynah recoil in fear. "For God's sake, Craig, don't do it! Don't shoot her! Stop, Craig, stop!" Then Zeke fired the gun, shooting Shaynah right in the chest.

The investigator dropped to the floor. Her head clunked loudly against the concrete. Zeke quickly ran over to her and shot her again, this time in the head. *Craig, thank you. Oh God, Craig, thank you!*

Zeke quickly leapt to the mattress. He grabbed the apron, which was still lying near the plate of uneaten cookies. He twisted the apron, jumped on top of Craig's body, and tied the apron around his neck. Then he pressed the gun roughly into Craig's outstretched hand. Zeke took off his gloves and threw them across the room.

"This is the police!" shouted a voice at the top of the stairs. "Drop all weapons!"

Zeke saw a face peer around the short wall at the top of the stairs. Then two cops stood next to each other on the upper part of the staircase, guns drawn.

"Put your hands up!" one cop yelled.

"I'm not armed!" Zeke yelled back. "Please help me! Please! I just killed him! He killed her, and I strangled him. I didn't mean to, but I didn't want him to kill me. Oh God, I can't believe this happened!"

"Identify yourself!"

"My name is Ezekiel Smith. I've been a prisoner down here for over a year! Please help me! Oh God, please help me! He shot her! I killed him! Oh God, please help me!"

PART III

37

ZEKE AND EZEKIEL

Zeke woke up in the same small room where he'd been sitting for the past eight hours or more. He was surprised that he had been able to get any sleep at all. He was sitting in an uncomfortable office chair. The room was brightly lit and contained only a small table with two chairs besides the one he was sitting in. It looked how he'd expected it would look. He'd already given a statement, but that was hours ago.

He got up from the chair and opened the door. He wasn't under arrest—yet—and had to go to the bathroom. A cop who was stationed right outside the door took Zeke down the hall and then escorted him immediately back to the small room when he was done. He was surprised at how sunny it had become outside already. Zeke didn't have his phone, and there wasn't a clock in the interview room.

He told the cop stationed at the door that he was hungry. After a few minutes, the cop returned with a bottle of water and a granola bar. Zeke was happy to have something to do while he waited. He was always aware of the camera in the corner of the room, recording all his movements and all his sounds. After finishing the granola bar, he got up and stretched. He did some push-ups and even stood on his head for a while, with his feet resting high against a wall. He was still wearing his black pants and shirt.

At some point, Detective Anders returned with another cop. So far, he'd been nice to Zeke. He was shorter than Zeke, older than Craig, and quite a bit heavier than both. The other cop was a young woman with her hair pulled back into a ponytail.

"How are you doing, Zeke?" Detective Anders asked.

"Can you call me Ezekiel?"

"Of course. You doing okay?" Anders asked again.

"Yeah, as well as can be expected. Can I go home yet?"

"Not yet. We still have some things that we want to clear up. Are you ready for a few more questions? It will help us to get the ball rolling so that we can get you out of here."

"Yeah, I'm ready," Zeke replied. "Go ahead."

"This is Detective Jerde. She's here to take notes and observe. So, Ezekiel, I just want to clear up a few things that we have questions about. Now first, you stated that you met Craig Kellerman when he was your manager at Geno's out by the mall. Then at some point, you moved into his house. Do you remember exactly when that was?"

"Yeah, the day after I graduated from high school."

"And you did that willingly."

"Well, not really. See—"

"You previously stated that you willingly moved in," Anders interrupted. "And I want you to know that we've talked with several of the neighbors. They all seem to think that you were always happy there. They didn't see any sign that you were captive."

"So at first, yeah, I moved in there willingly. We were having a relationship. But then he started holding me in the basement. He handcuffed me to the pipe in the corner."

"But you went running together—a lot. Couldn't you have escaped then?" Anders asked.

"Well," Zeke replied, "by that time, I guess I was having what you call Stockholm syndrome. I was really in love with my captor. I don't think the neighbors would have noticed. Craig only needed to chain me up at night. The rest of the time, I was happy to do whatever he ordered me to. I know now that I was really messed up. But at the time, it was like I wasn't able to think on my own, you know?"

"But you don't have any sign of injury on your wrist. We noticed at the crime scene—well, one of the crime scenes—that Craig Kellerman's wrist was pretty badly cut up. It was pretty raw. It looks like he was handcuffed at some point, for a long while. The medical examiner will do an autopsy soon, and they'll find out what caused the injury on his wrist. But my guess is that it's going to be handcuffs."

"That was because of sex. Yeah, it's really embarrassing to talk about, but he liked it when I'd handcuff him while we had sex."

"And you didn't try to escape when he was handcuffed?"

"Like I said, I have Stockholm syndrome. I didn't even realize that I could have escaped. And some of the time—I mean, most of the time, all the time—I was also handcuffed. We liked to handcuff each other."

"I also noticed," Anders continued, "that when I came down into the basement, you were wearing all black, the same clothes that you have on now, and Craig Kellerman was completely naked."

"So that's because we were having sex. We—"

"Okay," interrupted Anders, "this is going to be important. Let's take it slow. Let's go back to right before Shaynah Williams showed up at Craig's house. You know who Ms. Williams was, right?"

"I'm assuming she's the woman that Craig shot in the basement," Zeke replied. "I didn't know her name until now."

"Right. What were you doing just before she got to the house?"

"So like I said, Craig and I were in the basement, and we were having sex. We—"

"Were either of you handcuffed?" Anders interrupted.

"Um, no, not this time. I guess this was one of the rare times that we didn't get handcuffed. But we were having sex, and we were both naked."

"Why in the basement?"

"Craig had brought the mattress down there when he decided to hold me captive down there. So that's where the mattress was."

"Why not bring down the single mattress from the second bedroom? It's odd that he'd bring down the larger mattress from the master bedroom."

"I guess he wanted me to have more room, since I was uncomfortable from the handcuffs."

"Where did he sleep?"

"Oh, he always slept in the basement with me. That's why he brought the big mattress down there."

"Okay," Anders said, "so you guys are having sex ..."

"Yeah. We're going at it, and we hear the doorbell, right. Craig said just to ignore it, but it rang again. After a while, Craig said it was distracting and that I should go and see who it was."

"He wasn't worried about you escaping or asking for help?"

"No. I can see now that he realized how much he had me under his finger, I guess. He knew I wouldn't do anything wrong. So I got up and put on these black pants and shirt. They were the only clothes down there. Craig had lots of black clothes and gloves and things in the basement because that's where he prepared for his crimes."

"Where were your clothes?"

"Upstairs. We had started to have sex upstairs and got naked there, then moved to the mattress in the basement. Craig always kept his crime supplies down there, so when I went to see who was at the door, all I had to put on was the black stuff."

"And then you went upstairs. Did you take a weapon?"

"Nope. Just went up there. I saw the woman at the door. She said that she was from some sort of investigation thing, and she showed me a card. I thought she was a cop."

"Did she show you a badge?"

"No, but she had an official-looking card. I swear, I really thought she was a cop. And she was really aggressive. She said that she had some questions for Craig Kellerman and that I needed to bring her to him. She wouldn't take no for an answer."

"You must have told her he was home," said Anders.

"I did. She asked, and I'm not going to lie to a cop. So I said he was home."

"Did you tell her he was naked?"

"Yes—I mean no. Sorry. She was demanding to see him. So I yelled down to Craig, and he said it was okay to bring her down. I just assumed he'd put on some clothes—there are lots of black clothes down there."

"So she was in the house at this point?"

"Yeah, she followed me in. And when Craig said to bring her down, she just went down there. I followed her. That's when I saw that Craig was pointing the gun at her. Then I heard you guys coming in through the door, and I yelled at him not to shoot her. But he did. He shot her once in the chest, and she fell. Then he got up and shot her in the head."

"Where were you at this point?" Anders asked.

"I was on the stairs, behind the woman," Zeke replied. "But I was really scared that he was going to kill me. He had this wild look in his eyes. So while he was doing the shooting, I ran over to get behind him. I saw the apron on the floor and put it around his neck. I don't know where I got the strength because Craig was really strong. But I did. And I choked him to death. That's when you came down the stairs."

Detective Anders didn't say anything for several long minutes. He just looked at his paperwork and glanced through Detective Jerde's notes. Finally, Anders sighed loudly and said, "Well, Ezekiel, I'm just not buying it. Why didn't you run up the stairs when he started shooting?"

"Because—" Zeke began.

"No," Anders interrupted strongly, "it's not time for questions or answers right now. That was rhetorical. I'm just wondering why you didn't run up the stairs. Now, I've never choked a man to death, but I have had a man in a headlock. And let me tell you, it takes a long time to choke someone like that, especially someone as healthy as

Mr. Kellerman seems to have been. There are some real holes here. I can't let you go until we clear them up. Now you stated earlier that Craig Kellerman committed all the crimes in Duluth and Hibbing on his own. But Mrs. Kearney—she's the wife of the dead man in Hibbing—she says that there were two men, one of whom matches your description."

Detective Anders stood up and stepped toward the door. Jerde followed him.

"I'm just going to let all that sink in with you," Anders said as he opened the door. "We'll be back."

Several more hours passed. Zeke knew it had been this long because the sun was beginning to set when he asked to go to the bathroom for the fourth time. He hadn't eaten many calories since arriving at the police station, just two more granola bars and some water.

He spent the time stretching, sleeping, and singing "How Great Thou Art" to nobody. He wondered what was going on outside the station. He pictured all the newspeople clamoring for information about the suspect. He pictured Craig's house, surrounded by police tape, as investigators pored over every last inch.

Then there was a knock at the door. It opened, and a tall, well-built cop entered carrying a large folder. Zeke immediately noticed that he was quite attractive. He was about the same age as Craig. The cop closed the door and sat down at the table across from Zeke. He opened the folder and started ruffling through the papers.

"Okay," the cop said, "what do we have here? Mr. Smith, right?"

"Yeah," Zeke said as he sat straighter in his chair.

"I'm Sergeant Madson."

"What happened to Detective Anders?" Zeke asked.

"He's been working some long shifts and decided to take a break. So you're stuck with me for now. But we can see if we can get him back in here at some point. Now, Mr. Smith, is there anything I can get you right now? You comfortable?"

"I'm not really comfortable. But I'm okay, I guess. I am getting really hungry. When can I leave?"

"Well, that's entirely up to you. I'm not going to beat around the bush with you—I can tell that you don't like to waste time. Here's the deal: the sooner you tell us the truth, the sooner you can leave. Now I want to tell you that we've been talking to your parents—"

"My parents? You've actually talked to them?"

"Yes, sir. Your dad has been on the phone with us all day. They're all ready to welcome you back home as soon as we're done here. Your mom is already making your favorite dinner, even as we speak. But you see, we have a problem. We've got crime scene investigators up in Hibbing and at six different sites in Duluth, plus Craig Kellerman's home, so that's eight crime scenes. There's a lot of information all coming into this station. Now of course, anything that requires a lab report is still out—you know, DNA tests and fingerprints, stuff like that. But we've got a whole lot of other evidence that is starting to tell us a pretty good story. We need you to verify the story and fill in a few blank spaces. We need that so that we can give the families, and all the people involved in this, some peace. Understand?"

"Yes, of course," Zeke said. "That's what I want too."

"Great," Madson replied. "So let's get this thing started. Now tell me, how did Dan Kearney die up there in Hibbing?"

"I don't have any idea. I wasn't there."

"Mrs. Kearney said that there were two people in her home. We've traced the crime through some cameras to a car that was rented with a stolen identity—a crime that Shaynah Williams recently tracked to Craig Kellerman. We also know that the Kearneys had lunch at Geno's earlier that day and that they had some sort of argument with you. Now that's quite a coincidence. We have the footage of you serving the Kearneys their lunch. Then we've got Kellerman talking to them. And we've got the car. So, Mr. Smith, how did Dan Kearney die?"

"Maybe Craig killed him, I guess."

"Yeah, could be. Except that Mrs. Kearney recognized his voice. See, Craig got her talking about a book that was on her nightstand while you were out of the room with her husband. After she found out about the Geno's connection, she told us that she's absolutely positive that the manager stayed with her in the bedroom while the server killed her husband downstairs—all while her children were sleeping nearby. So again, how did Dan Kearney die?"

"Craig must have picked up someone else. I really don't know. I'm being honest here—I just don't know what else to tell you. Craig knew a lot of people—there were a lot of other servers my age at the restaurant. You don't want me to lie, do you?"

"Of course not. Remember, you can go home when you start telling the truth. However, right now, your answers don't match what the crime scene is telling us. And we're still talking about Hibbing— we've got a lot more to talk about that happened right here in Duluth."

Sergeant Madson got up from the table and walked to the door. Then he turned. "I'm stepping out for a bit," Madson said. "You've got some things to think about. Just keep in mind that this can go good for you or very bad for you. The best way to make it go good is to tell us the truth—to tell us the events that match the evidence we have. I'll be back in a bit."

By this point, Zeke had lost all sense of time. He knew it was completely dark outside. He passed the time by working out with sit-ups and push-ups. He spent a lot of time standing on his head. He continued to sing "How Great Thou Art" and to take periodic naps on the floor.

Again, there was a knock at the door, and Sergeant Madson entered. Madson sat at the table and opened his folder.

Zeke was on the floor when he entered. He immediately got up and sat in his chair.

"I'm sorry that it took so long," Madson said. "There's just a lot going on out there. Really, you should see it. It's a complete circus. So how are you doing?"

"I've been thinking a lot," Zeke replied. "And I'm ready to tell the truth. I just want to go home—to my parents' home, not Craig's—and get something to eat."

"That sounds like a very good idea. Now how did Dan Kearney die?"

"I shot him," Zeke said bluntly.

Madson sat back in his chair, sighed loudly, and said, "Ezekiel, I thought we'd come to an understanding. And now you're still lying to me. How did Dan Kearney die?"

"I can't really remember. I know I killed him. Maybe I strangled him?"

"With what?"

"My hands?"

"You couldn't strangle someone with your hands. It had to be something you brought with you. Now we know you had a gun and some zip ties that Kellerman used on Mrs. Kearney—and a knife that she saw you holding."

"Oh, I stabbed him," said Zeke.

Sergeant Madson got up from the table and closed his folder. "I'll come back when you've had time to remember what really happened."

"Okay!" Zeke shouted. "I'll tell you. I strangled him with a zip tie—just don't leave. Let me finish—I strangled him with a zip tie!"

Madson opened the door, stuck his head out into the hall, and said, "Hey, can you get us a pizza? Mr. Smith and I are really hungry. What do you want, Ezekiel, pepperoni? A Coke?"

"Yeah," Zeke said, "pepperoni and a Diet Coke."

"You like Bulldog Pizza?" Sergeant Madson asked.

38

THE TRUTH WILL SET YOU FREE

It was the Christmas before the events in Hibbing and Duluth. Craig and Zeke were lying in bed together. They'd just had sex and were now talking about an episode of *Forensic Files*.

"I know how I'd do it," said Craig. "I know exactly how I'd get away with murder. Here's how it all goes down. First, the cops will bring me in because, for whatever reason, they suspect me. They've probably got some evidence against me—I have to realize that. So I go in. But—and this is really important—I don't ask for a lawyer. That's key to how this all works.

"I sit there in the interrogation room and keep denying it. Over and over again, I deny it. I have to come up with some alternative story that doesn't have to be perfect, just a tad plausible. They keep on me for hours. I keep denying it. But you see, they have evidence against me, or they wouldn't have brought me in. They keep throwing that evidence against me. But I let them do it. I have to make it go on for hours. The whole thing is being taped. I have to remember not to rush it—I want the tape to show that it took many hours for all this to happen.

"Now, after a good eight or nine hours, I appear really tired and worn out. I say that I'm really hungry and tired and want to go home—I want to get that on tape. They'll start to leak to me whatever evidence they have. I'll start to break. Now—here is the really smart part—I start to confess, little by little. I keep letting them feed me the evidence and their version of the story. Hell, it will probably be pretty close to what I actually did—the detectives likely won't be idiots. They'll have done their jobs, and I'll let them do it. And at the end of the interrogation, I'll have given them a full confession. I just have to be very careful to let them bring up anything specific. I have to let them suggest a weapon—then I can confess that I used it.

"Now it's time to get a lawyer. But I tell that attorney that I didn't do it—the police made me give a false confession. I go back to the original story and swear my innocence. I keep telling them that I was tired and confused and that the police just wouldn't let me rest. I'll say that I was hungry and not thinking right. I just keep going back to my original story and say that the confession was forced. They'll get the tapes of the interrogation. The tapes will show how long it took. I won't stop saying that I gave the confession so that the police would just let me go.

"It will go to trial because, after all, they actually do have evidence against me. But at trial, my lawyer will defend me by saying that I gave a false confession. My lawyers will just keep hammering that point—the police are bad and just wanted to get the first guy they could find. The police were so hungry to get someone that they cooked up any evidence they did have, and then they coerced a confession out of me. They made me hungry and tired. I was helpless and a victim of the police.

"All I need is one juror to have watched some of those true-crime shows. I just need one person to believe that I was coerced into giving a false confession. It'll probably be a liberal-minded woman. Maybe there will be more, but I just need one. And don't forget, I'll have already planted an alternative version of the crime where I didn't do it. The one person who believes me won't be able to vote guilty because they'll feel that they are smarter and better than the cops. They'll feel terrible that I was put through the interrogation.

"That's it. The jury comes back either hung or innocent. I've just gotten away with murder. But here's the brilliant part: I did it by telling the truth."

39

A CHURCH DIVIDED

After the horrific 1977 murders of Elizabeth Congdon and her nurse at the Glensheen mansion in Duluth, Elizabeth's own daughter and son-in-law were arrested for the crimes and granted separate trials. However, both defense teams were doubtful that the pair could get fair trials in St. Louis County. St. Louis County was the largest county, geographically, in Minnesota and one of the largest in the country, stretching from Duluth to the Canadian border and encompassing most of Minnesota's Iron Range, including the city of Hibbing.

The Glensheen murder trials, as they became known, were moved to Hastings, the seat of Dakota County. Hastings was a river town that sat twenty miles down the Mississippi from St. Paul. At the time of the Glensheen murder trials, it was a small rural community. By the time Ezekiel Smith's trial was moved there, Hastings had become much more suburban.

Considerable debate had occurred in St. Louis County over the prospect of moving the Ezekiel Smith trial out of the county. Many felt that since the crimes were so horrendous in nature and impacted the entire region, the citizens of the county had a right to seek justice in their own territory. However, Zeke's defense team was able to prove that it would be virtually impossible to find an impartial jury in the area. In the end, the county prosecutors conceded. They were concerned that any unfairness from the jury would lead to an appeal or mistrial.

Zeke was formally charged with five counts of first-degree murder, one count of manslaughter, and seven counts of burglary with a deadly weapon. The first-degree murders included those of Dan Kearney of Hibbing, Hank Neilson of Duluth, Anna Carlson and her grandson Tucker of Duluth, and Shaynah Williams of St. Paul. An arduous and gut-wrenching week of consideration had led the county prosecutor to lower the charge for the murder of Craig Kellerman to manslaughter. Several factors played into this decision, but basically, he made this call just in case the jury believed Zeke had really been a captive.

It took an entire year for both the prosecution and defense to prepare. Zeke had no money of his own. However, in an act of unforeseen generosity, Zeke's parents took out a second mortgage on their home and liquidated all their other assets to provide their son with a team of lawyers from Minneapolis. They truly believed that Ezekiel had been taken and corrupted by a militant homosexual. There was no way, in their eyes, that their son would have done the things he was charged with.

An unlikely force joined the conservative, religious Smiths in supporting Zeke. Many in the gay community believed that due to his dogmatic upbringing, Ezekiel had been an easy target for an unstable and older gay man. Their hearts went out to him. Only a situation this strange could make it possible for the conservative religious folks to be on the same side as the bleeding-heart gay liberals.

But not everyone was on their side. The Ezekiel Smith trial tore through the emotions of many in Minnesota and the upper Midwest. The news media had been relentless in giving out as much information as they could—whether it had been properly vetted or not. By the time of the trial, very few were undecided or remained in the middle. To one set of people, Zeke was a cold-blooded killer who had acted alone after killing Craig Kellerman. To the rest of the people, Zeke had been imprisoned while Craig Kellerman committed the crimes, and then he had become a hero by strangling Kellerman to death in an attempt to save his own life.

Lake Superior Celebration Church lost around 30 percent of its congregation. Those who stayed believed that their pastor's son was a kindhearted boy who had mistaken Satan for a man offering a helping hand. These same people put most of the blame on a police force that was incapable of handling a complex investigation and instead had forced its first suspect to confess. They were also committed to the idea that the police had planted evidence that simply didn't exist.

The other side of the population held just as strongly to their belief that Ezekiel Smith was a homicidal psychopath. They did not entertain thoughts about the effects of growing up gay in a religious family. After all, they proclaimed, many people grew up gay in conservative households and didn't become killers. These people wanted to see Zeke locked up and the key thrown away. Their biggest regret was that Minnesota did not have the death penalty.

40

HE DID IT

Finally, after more than a year of preparation and practice, it was Marilyn Richards's day to shine. She had worked as a prosecutor in St. Louis County for seventeen years. She and her colleague formed the two-person team that represented the people of Minnesota in the *State of Minnesota v. Ezekiel Smith*.

Seven weeks earlier, her colleague had given the opening statement for the prosecution. Now, after twenty-eight witnesses and seventy-three exhibits, it was Marilyn's turn to give the closing argument. She was in her mid-fifties and would use all her experience to convince twelve people that she and the state of Minnesota were right—that Ezekiel Smith belonged behind bars for the rest of his life.

"Ladies and gentlemen of the jury," Marilyn said as she stood and moved to the podium in front of the jury box, "on behalf of St. Louis County, I want to thank you for all your time and attention. We understand that you don't live in our county of pine forests, iron mines, and giant lakes. In a way, you are tasked with considering a situation that belongs to some other people. But in a sense, all juries of murder trials work on behalf of someone else—because, ladies and gentlemen, you are not working for the citizens of your own Dakota County or for the citizens of your northern cousins in St. Louis

County. You are working on behalf of the men and women who can't be in the courtroom today because they are dead.

"Now, you've heard from lots of people over the past seven weeks. You've even heard from Mr. Smith, the defendant, himself in the form of a taped confession. And yes, it is the state's absolute belief that Mr. Smith gave a complete and accurate confession while being in full control of his capacities. Also, it was a confession that he signed in his own handwriting.

"However, as important as his confession is, let's set it aside for several minutes. You see, there is a truth in the form of a chain of events that the evidence gives us. What is evidence? Sure, on a base level it's the footprints and the camera footage and the computer files and countless other items. But these are just the form of the evidence. What, exactly, is evidence? Evidence is the victims speaking to us from beyond their graves.

"The victims who are deceased no longer have a voice, but they can still speak to us—loudly. Through evidence they cry out and tell you their story. Ladies and gentlemen of the jury, it's now your job to listen to their story.

"Everything began with Craig Kellerman. Both sides in this case agree that Mr. Kellerman was a deeply troubled human being without a normal system of values. He had an absolute obsession with committing the perfect crime. But Mr. Kellerman is not here to face his own charges. And in a way, it's quite ironic that you are being asked to seek justice for his death when, at the same time, we know that he wasn't the best of people.

"Allegedly—and we must use that word because he will never stand trial for his crimes—Mr. Kellerman broke into a museum in Walnut Grove, Minnesota, and took Laura Ingalls Wilder's quilt. This quilt was worthless to him. It was old, didn't provide much warmth, and would have been impossible to liquidate for any sort of elevated price. But Mr. Kellerman wanted it just to have it. He went on to steal Charles Lindbergh's first toy airplane, the urn that had once held Sinclair Lewis's ashes, and the Kensington Runestone. Of all these items, only the urn has been recovered. It was discovered in Kellerman's home. As soon as this trial is over, that urn will be returned to the good people of Sauk Centre in Stearns County.

"So it all began with Craig Kellerman. We heard from Karen O'Neil, the owner of Geno's Restaurant in Duluth. She told us that Craig met Ezekiel Smith while Smith was working as a server. Kellerman was a manager. Ms. O'Neil stated that these two men were great friends, and as she said, wherever you saw one, you saw the other.

"On the day after he graduated from high school, Mr. Smith moved into Craig Kellerman's house in Duluth. By all accounts, they lived a happy and normal life. You heard the testimony of neighbors who saw the men running together. They also saw Mr. Smith mowing the lawn alone. Not one witness testified that there was any sort of abnormal circumstances surrounding the two men. Not one neighbor believed that anyone had been a prisoner.

"Let's take a side trip for a moment and talk about the testimony of defense psychiatrist Dr. Christopher Kromminga. Dr. Kromminga testified that Ezekiel Smith grew up in an extremely conservative and religious household. He called it abusive. And ladies and gentlemen, it probably was. I believe it was very, very difficult for Mr. Smith to grow up under the circumstances that we heard about. So the evidence that Dr. Kromminga presented is absolutely a fact: Ezekiel Smith grew up as a gay person in a conservative and hostile environment. It's not Dr. Kromminga's evidence that I dispute; it's his interpretation of the impact. Dr. Kromminga went on to state that Mr. Smith's upbringing made him easily fall prey to Stockholm syndrome with Mr. Kellerman. That interpretation is an opinion; it's not based on fact. In fact, there are many, many gay people right in this state who grew up inside religious and conservative homes—these people did not grow up to defend the reprehensible acts of another or go on to commit reprehensible acts themselves. These people did not grow up and fall prey, easily, to domineering personalities. Once again, not one witness testified that they observed Mr. Smith being held as a prisoner by Mr. Kellerman.

"Let's go back to the two men inside that house. We don't know too much about what occurred during the year they lived together. Remember, we are letting the evidence speak. We cannot make up things that don't exist. And so we just don't know what daily life was like for the two men in the house, except we know that they went to work—Mr. Smith worked more than Mr. Kellerman—and that they committed many acts of identify theft while working at Geno's Restaurant. We also know, from Mr. Smith's recorded confession, that the two men had sex often. And while having sex they liked to tie each other up with handcuffs.

"How do we know about Craig Kellerman's museum thefts and the credit card thefts that followed? We know because Shaynah Williams hunted down the evidence for us before she met her untimely and horrible death in Kellerman's basement. Remember Mark Peterson? Shaynah Williams's investigation partner? He told us that Ms. Williams was a dedicated forensic investigator who would not let this case die. Even when she was given other projects and was told that the museum thefts were no longer a priority, she continued to work on her own time to track down the items. She was a hero to the people of this state.

"But back to the end of the first year of Smith and Kellerman living together: You saw the evidence that the Duluth Police Department collected from the Kellerman home. These men had been preparing for a crime wave for quite some time. You saw the tools and drugs and clothing and weapons—all stored away for the future perfect crime. It was just a matter of when and where that first crime would be.

"I won't forget the testimony of Mrs. Kearney, and I know that none of you in the jury box will forget it either. She was heartbroken and distraught—as a young widow should be. She told us about that first day of the crime spree. She, her husband, and their two children drove to Duluth for shopping. They stopped at Geno's Restaurant for lunch and had an argument with their server, Ezekiel Smith. You saw the camera footage of this occurrence. And you saw that Mr. Kellerman spoke with them. But that's not all you saw. When the Kearney family left and drove back to Hibbing, you saw footage, from various cameras, of Kellerman's car following them to their home.

"The evidence continues to tell us that Kellerman drove back to Duluth and rented a car with a stolen credit card and identity. At some point, he picked up Mr. Smith, and they drove to Hibbing. They broke into the Kearney home in the middle of the night, causing untold stress to the Kearneys. Mrs. Kearney told us that Kellerman tied her up in the bedroom while Smith went with her husband to get some money—only there was just forty dollars in the house. So Smith, upset at having only forty dollars to show for his crime, murdered Dan Kearney by tying a zip tie around his neck. Dan Kearney died in the laundry room while his two boys, ages two and four, slept upstairs. He was thirty-four years old.

"The two men drove back to Duluth with their forty dollars and returned their car. But now something strange occurred. Smith used handcuffs to chain Kellerman to a pipe in the basement of the house. We don't know why. Remember, we are listening to the evidence and cannot make up anything that we can't prove. So we simply don't know why Ezekiel turned on Craig Kellerman. We can surmise that perhaps Kellerman was upset about the murder and was threatening to turn Smith into the police—we can surmise that, but we can't know that. However, we can absolutely know that Kellerman, not Smith, was handcuffed for multiple days in the basement. We know this because the medical examiner sat right in that chair and told us that Kellerman's wrist was so badly wounded, it had to have been under trauma for at least two days.

"And now comes that horrible second night of the spree. Smith, alone, left the house. You saw footage from various cameras that tracked his car. He started with Mrs. Edy McCabe, age eighty-four. He broke in, threatened her at gunpoint, and made off with five thousand dollars of her hard-earned money. You got to hear this evidence from Mrs. McCabe herself. She's one of the lucky ones—she's still around to tell the facts.

"Mr. Hank Neilson is not around, unfortunately. He's not around because he had only two hundred dollars in his home. You heard testimony that Mr. Neilson was a bit paranoid and put a small mark on all his bills. Two hundred dollars of those marked bills were found in the Kellerman home. If he'd had more, he might have been allowed to live. But that wasn't the case. Smith cut a screen and entered the home. When there wasn't enough money, just like in the case of Dan Kearney, Smith flipped and shot Hank Neilson in the head.

"The next home on Ezekiel Smith's tour of Duluth belonged to Sarah Dockindorf. Ms. Dockindorf was lucky—she slept through the whole thing. She ended up losing $7,220 and her sense of security, but at least she is alive to tell about it.

"Mr. Smith went back to Kellerman's house. The evidence tells us that Kellerman was still alive and chained in the basement. It was now the next day. Nothing happened, that the evidence tells us, until Smith got a pizza from Bulldog Pizza around dinnertime. Now we've come to the third, final, and most horrific night of the crime spree—this would be the second night in Duluth.

"It begins with Lisa Sumner. She wasn't home. Now here is one woman who is very glad she was working late into the evening. She only lost eighteen hundred dollars and got to keep her life.

"Charles Hendricks likes to sleep with a fan on. He didn't hear anything, but then he woke up and found that his life's savings, all fifteen thousand dollars of it, had disappeared. Now you can think what you want about the safety of keeping that much money in cash in your home. But it was his right to do so. And it was taken from him. You heard him testify that he had to move because he can't trust living in his beloved house any longer. Often, loss of cash takes second place to the loss of dignity.

"Dignity. I shudder to even mention that word as I think about our next victims, the Carlsons. We have no way of knowing how much money, if any, Mr. Smith was able to get from Anna Carlson.

She was seventy-two, a widow, babysitting her grandson Tucker. The evidence tells us that Smith shot Anna Carlson first. The evidence does not tell us why. Maybe she didn't provide enough money. But whatever the reason, the evidence tells us that Tucker, age eleven, was beaten to death with a candlestick shortly after his grandma died.

"You saw the candlestick that was found in the Kellerman home. You saw the gun. You heard from the weapons expert who testified about the bullets found in the bodies and how they absolutely came from the specific gun that was found in the Kellerman house—but not until after it claimed one more victim.

"Now, after the horrible slaying of the Carlson boy, Smith went back to Kellerman's house. It was morning already. The evidence tells us that at some point Smith made cookies and then strangled Kellerman to death with an apron. You heard the testimony of the medical examiner—Craig Kellerman died well before Shaynah Williams set foot on the property. You also heard the medical examiner tell us that Kellerman had ketamine in his blood. Ketamine is a powerful drug used to incapacitate people. There was a box of syringes full of ketamine in the Kellerman basement. Ezekiel Smith would not have been able to suffocate someone as strong as Craig Kellerman without some help. The evidence tells us that Ezekiel Smith injected Kellerman with the drug, waited for him to pass out, and then strangled him with the apron. In fact, we learned that Smith's prints were on the ketamine syringe—not Kellerman's. Let's be clear about this: Mr. Smith killed Mr. Kellerman deliberately after injecting him with a drug that incapacitated him.

"At this point, Ms. Williams—our hero—was closing in on Kellerman and Smith. She'd been up to Geno's Restaurant and had obtained enough evidence to support the claim that Kellerman had been stealing the identities of the restaurant's customers. She went to question him. The defense would have you believe that Ms. Williams was invited down to the basement, where she went willingly. That is not what happened. We don't have evidence to prove this point, but we do have the ability to rely on Ms. Williams's extensive training and knowledge of crime. She would never have stepped foot into that house without a police escort.

"Here is what really happened. Smith forced Williams inside with the gun. He took her down to the basement, where she assuredly saw Craig Kellerman's dead body. When he heard the Duluth police arrive upstairs, Smith shot Shaynah Williams twice and placed the blame on Craig Kellerman. Then Smith completed his farce by pretending to strangle Kellerman—an act he'd already accomplished hours before. This is the only scenario that fits with the evidence. Every other scenario presented in this courtroom conflicts with at least one piece of evidence. The narrative I have given you just now is the only possible truth that fits with every piece of evidence.

"And here we are today. Let the victims speak to you. Hear their voices through the evidence. The events that I have just laid out for you make a cohesive truth that is scientifically supported through testimony and the exhibits entered into this court. And behind all of this scientific fact is the additional fact that Ezekiel Smith confessed to all the crimes before this court.

"I have a responsibility to work for the people of St. Louis County. You have a responsibility to work for the victims. There is no doubting the actual evidence. You must return seven guilty verdicts for burglary with a deadly weapon, one guilty verdict for the manslaughter of Craig Kellerman, and five guilty verdicts for the gruesome and cold-blooded first-degree murders of Dan Kearney, Hank Neilson, Anna Carlson, and her young grandson Tucker, who never had a chance to live, and finally, our hero, Shaynah Williams.

"Ladies and gentlemen of the jury, Your Honor, the people of St. Louis County now rest."

41

DARROW TAKES
A TURN

Every state, along with the federal government, dictates that the prosecution goes last in the delivery of closing arguments at trial—every state except one, that is. In Minnesota, the defense always has the last word.

Kurt Feirri was the third generation in a powerhouse law firm in Minneapolis. He was a large man in height, weight, and personality. He didn't like suits because they were uncomfortable. Throughout the trial, he'd worn casual dress pants and brightly colored shirts. He liked expensive watches and cheap cologne.

Mr. Feirri stood to give his closing argument. He approached the podium in front of the jury box. However, before he began to speak, he took all the pages of his argument and ripped them in two—right in front of the jury. Then he dropped the pieces on the floor and went to the microphone.

"Members of the jury, I had a whole statement ready to read to you. However, as I sat and listened to Ms. Richards, I knew that I just couldn't stand here and read what I had written a few days ago. I couldn't let her distort your truth right before you are to make one of the most important decisions you will ever make. So forgive me for ripping my pages, but I feel the need to speak from my heart.

"You see, I'm passionate about this case. I was passionate about it the day that I met Ezekiel Smith. And I'm not going to waste any more of your time. Enough time has been wasted already on this trial. But I had to rip up my speech because Ms. Richards cannot be allowed to taint the evidence. It's just not fair to Ezekiel Smith, a very nice young man who was caught in a terrible situation. It's also not fair to the victims of these terrible crimes. Remember, if you convict the wrong person, then the right person is still out there and needs to be caught. Letting Ms. Richards taint the evidence is not fair to any of us.

"Evidence, evidence—how many times did Prosecutor Richards say the word 'evidence' during her closing argument? Too many to count. Yes, evidence is extremely important. But it means nothing without an understanding of the context in which it exists.

"Members of the jury, there is absolutely no evidence that ties Ezekiel Smith to any of the crime scenes—with the exception of what occurred inside Craig Kellerman's house, and we will get to that. Let me say that again: in all the crime scenes in Hibbing and Duluth, there is not any evidence that places Ezekiel Smith anywhere near the crimes.

"But let's start with Hibbing. Yep, Mrs. Kearney testified and told us of her horrible ordeal. My heart goes out to her—it really does. She suffered terribly and lost her husband, all while her children slept down the hall. However, you also heard that she could not identity Ezekiel Smith in a photo lineup. The police tried, but she couldn't do it. Why? Because she never saw the second assailant's face. It could have been anyone that Craig Kellerman found. Again, there is absolutely no evidence to tie Mr. Smith to the crimes in Hibbing. Kellerman rented the car through a stolen identify. Two men are pictured on some traffic cameras, but they can't be identified.

"And I'd also like you to remember that we heard testimony from one of the Kearneys' neighbors. Mrs. Kearney made a post to their neighborhood social media site that said, and I quote, 'These homosexuals are ruining this country. I'm going to make sure that Smith burns. I don't care whether he did it or not. These homosexuals have to learn that we are going to fight back,' end of quote. Now, again, my heart goes out to her for everything that happened to her that night. But she is, in her own words, an unreliable witness.

"Now I'd like to talk about Dr. Kromminga, the psychiatrist who testified. Dr. Kromminga spent a lot of time with Ezekiel. Let me remind you that Dr. Kromminga is a leading expert in the field of childhood psychological trauma caused by growing up gay. Ms. Richards attacked the doctor's interpretation of his findings. I find this reprehensible. Dr. Kromminga never said that all gay children grow up to be victims of Stockholm syndrome. He never said that. What he said was that children who grow up gay in extremely religious households have a higher chance of being susceptible to persuasive individuals—and that this higher chance of susceptibility often includes a form of Stockholm syndrome. That's what he said. That is the evidence in his testimony.

"Also, Dr. Kromminga testified that he performed a full battery of psychological tests on Mr. Smith. And with his years and years of professional experience, Dr. Kromminga concluded that Ezekiel Smith was absolutely a victim of Stockholm syndrome.

"Of course, the neighbors never noticed that anything was wrong. Ezekiel did every single thing that Craig Kellerman ever asked of him. They were, from all outside appearances, an absolutely perfect couple. But these neighbors were not inside the house, where Ezekiel was being chained to a pipe night after night.

"Ms. Richards forgot to mention the expert testimony of Dr. Sanchez. Dr. Sanchez, a wound expert, testified that it is very possible that Ezekiel was constrained with the handcuffs we found in the basement of Kellerman's house. She inspected these exact handcuffs and fit them around Ezekiel's wrist. Ezekiel's wrists are much smaller than those of Craig Kellerman. Dr. Sanchez told us that it's quite possible, and even likely, that Ezekiel Smith could have worn these handcuffs every night for an entire year without showing even the smallest scratch.

"Now we know that Craig Kellerman had a wound on his wrist. But remember that Dr. Sanchez told us that wound was consistent with a one-time injury resulting from a rope used during a sex act. It was the medical examiner who told us that Kellerman's injury came from the handcuffs. But the medical examiner is not a wound expert with years of experience studying just wounds—Dr. Sanchez is this expert, and she told us that Craig Kellerman's wrist was, once again, injured by a rope in a one-time sex act. We found the rope in the basement, and we showed it to you. Craig Kellerman was never handcuffed as a prisoner. Ezekiel Smith was.

"Members of the jury, not one of the surviving witnesses could positively identify Ezekiel Smith from a photo lineup. Neither could they identify Craig Kellerman. Now, we know that someone in the Kellerman house committed all those terrible crimes, including the murder of the young grandson, Tucker. It's terrible—terrible. We know that someone in the Kellerman house did it because the murder weapons were found in the house, along with black clothing and blood samples that belonged to the victims. However, unfortunately, no blood or any DNA belonging to either Craig Kellerman or Ezekiel Smith has been found anywhere. One of these two men committed the crimes. But which one? Without conclusive evidence, we must look at the circumstances around the men.

"Ms. Richards told you her version of the story. She said it was based on evidence. But she didn't point out all the evidence that doesn't exist. Where is any evidence connecting Ezekiel Smith to any crime? There isn't any because it doesn't exist. And so, if we know that someone in the house did these things, and we have no evidence as to who, then we must look at the circumstances surrounding the two men. That's what we're going to do now as I tell you what really occurred.

"Ezekiel Smith grew up the son of a conservative pastor in Duluth, Minnesota. He was a good kid. Got really good grades. Was never in trouble a day in his life. Many people in the family's church say that Ezekiel is a very nice guy. However, not all was good with Ezekiel. He was born gay. It happens. Let me tell you, people of the jury, that I was born gay. And let me tell you that often it sucks—for lack of a better word. Families don't always understand. Mine wasn't too bad, but my dad was an attorney with lots of gay clients—he wasn't a minister like Ezekiel Smith's father. But life was still not great for me when I was growing up. I can't imagine how hard it was for the defendant.

"But despite all that, Ezekiel grew up and graduated from a Christian high school with honors. He had a job. We learned from testimony in this trial that Ezekiel got a job so that he could donate money and help people. Does that sound like a killer? Not to me.

"Ezekiel worked as a server at Geno's Restaurant in Duluth. He was good at it. You heard how much the owner of the restaurant liked Zeke, as she called him, and she said he was a model employee. However, also working at this restaurant was a manager named Craig Kellerman.

"Now this is something that I entirely agree with Ms. Richards on—Craig Kellerman was a terrible man. Just awful. He was obsessed with crime. He had been planning crimes for years. But he was missing a crucial item—something he needed desperately to commit a perfect crime. He was missing an accomplice. So he looked around the restaurant, and there was Ezekiel Smith. Smith was a young, very attractive guy with a likable personality. Craig Kellerman started to groom Ezekiel Smith from the first day he met him—yes, groomed, every single day. By the time Ezekiel graduated from high school, he had no ability to resist the charms of Craig Kellerman. Now remember, Ezekiel was eighteen at the time. He was a virgin and had never even masturbated. And here comes Craig Kellerman. You all saw his photographs. He was very good-looking. I'm not going to beat around the bush here—Ezekiel was an eighteen-year-old male virgin who was horny as hell. Add to that the fact that he had been groomed by Kellerman since day one, and you don't need a psychiatrist to tell you that Ezekiel Smith fell deeply in love, and lust, with Kellerman.

"So Smith moves into the Kellerman home. They have sex—a lot. It escalates and gets kinky. But Ezekiel isn't going to do anything to disappoint the only person who has ever shown him attention and love in this way. But then the Stockholm syndrome takes hold—and it takes hold strongly. Ezekiel is handcuffed to a pipe in the basement night after night. Sure, during the day, the two men go running. They go to work. They mow the lawn and go grocery shopping. But members of the jury, that is exactly what Stockholm syndrome is— it's abuse that the victim doesn't realize is happening. Ezekiel wasn't going to do anything to change the situation because he thought this was how it was supposed to be—he thought that this was love.

"Sad. So sad to think about. Put yourself in his place. You've lived two decades without another human showing you any interest, and then here comes this unbelievably good-looking guy. Yes, that's all it took.

"Kellerman, who had already committed acts of extreme theft, went to Hibbing to stick it to the Kearneys because they'd given him a rough time at the restaurant. He rented a car and took an accomplice. But that accomplice was not Ezekiel Smith. Who was it? We don't know. Why? Because there is absolutely no evidence to tell us, and the one person who did know, Craig Kellerman, is dead. It could have been any number of men from around the area. Hell, without evidence, it could have been any guy of the same height and weight on the planet.

"Kellerman comes back to the house and goes out for two more nights of unspeakable madness. He's a ruthless maniac who kills without any regard for humanity. Do you really think that a man such as Kellerman would have allowed himself to be tied up while a nineteen-year-old with no experience did these things? It doesn't make sense. And since we have no evidence to prove that Ezekiel Smith was at any of the crime scenes, we have to understand that if it doesn't make sense, then it simply isn't true.

"Oh! And then there was the part of the trial when we saw my favorite witness of the entire case. The prosecution called Mrs. Faye Ocala to the stand. Remember her? She was Ezekiel Smith's sixth-grade teacher. You might not remember her because she was only on the stand for forty-five seconds of testimony. In fact, she gave such ludicrous testimony that Ms. Richards didn't even bother to mention her in the prosecution's closing argument. Mrs. Ocala testified that Ezekiel Smith was obsessed with the Glensheen murders. That was her entire testimony—that a sixth-grade Ezekiel Smith was obsessed. Well, I ask you, members of the jury, what sixth-grade boy in Duluth isn't obsessed with the Glensheen murders? None of you live in Duluth. But let me tell you, if you live in Duluth, you are used to driving by that enormous old mansion a lot. And every time you drive past, someone is bound to comment on the murders. If Ezekiel Smith is guilty because he was interested in Glensheen, then we have to take a look at half the population of northern Minnesota!

"Now Ms. Richards and I agree that Shaynah Williams was a hero. She went way above and beyond to track down a criminal. When she did, unfortunately, she ended up being killed by Craig Kellerman, after being lured into his basement. But her death was not in vain. Her death lit a flame inside Ezekiel Smith, and it was then that Ezekiel had enough strength to end the madness that was Craig Kellerman. It took tremendous courage for Ezekiel to overcome his Stockholm syndrome and save himself from Kellerman—Shaynah Williams gave him that courage.

"Yes, everyone in this courtroom, including Ezekiel Smith himself, will tell you that Ezekiel Smith killed Craig Kellerman. But was this an act of manslaughter? No! This was self-defense. As soon as Kellerman finished with Shaynah Williams, he would have turned the gun on Ezekiel. If he wanted to live, Ezekiel had no choice but to grab whatever he could find and strangle Kellerman with every last ounce of strength in his body. Just think about it! If Ezekiel Smith had killed Craig Kellerman earlier in the day, with all the time in the world, why the hell would he have done it with an old apron?

"Let's talk about the ketamine that Ms. Richards mentioned in her argument. We've got ketamine in Kellerman's blood. We've got a syringe in the basement. The syringe has ketamine on the inside and Ezekiel Smith's fingerprints on the outside. Again, if we look at just the evidence, then it doesn't look good for Mr. Smith. However, you heard from Dr. Sanchez, the wound expert. With many years of experience, Dr. Sanchez informed us that the ketamine puncture wound occurred well before Kellerman died. In fact, the medical examiner found multiple syringe wounds on Kellerman's body. He must have been a drug addict. Don't forget the testimony of Dr. Ron Louis, the psychiatrist who specializes in addictions. He told us that ketamine is a drug that is abused by many people. He also stated that ketamine is used by some people during sex. And we know from the forensic report that Craig Kellerman's prints were also on the syringe. When we take this evidence and put it together, we can conclude that Kellerman was an addict who liked to use ketamine during sex. When they were having sex, Kellerman ordered Ezekiel to get a syringe of ketamine—that's why Ezekiel's prints are on the syringe.

"Now let's talk about what makes sense with the evidence and what does not. The medical examiner assures us that Craig Kellerman was strangled with an apron that was tied around his neck. Earlier in the day, Ezekiel Smith would have had an entire cabinet of weapons to use to kill Craig Kellerman. So why did he choose an apron? Because an apron was the only item, other than a bunch of cookies, that was close enough when Kellerman was shooting Shaynah Williams. It would have made no sense for Ezekiel to kill Kellerman earlier in the day with an old apron. If it doesn't make sense, then it isn't true.

"This brings us to the confession. People of the jury, I find it extremely odd that Prosecutor Richards spent less than ten total seconds discussing the confession during her entire closing argument. That should tell you something. You see, according the prosecution, the confession is the cornerstone of Ezekiel's guilt. If this confession is that important, then why was it hardly ever mentioned? I'll tell you why—because that confession was coerced by an all-too-eager police department hell-bent on arresting the first homosexual they could find.

"We all sat in this courtroom together and watched the tapes of the interrogation. And let me assure you, that's what it was—an interrogation. I was sick to my stomach—I still am when I think about it. No sleep. Ezekiel Smith was given no chance to sleep or relax. You saw how he was acting in that room—he was singing and stretching and finding any way he could to stay awake and pass the time. Hours went by when he didn't see anyone. He was given water and three granola bars. You should go home and try to live an entire day—the most stressful day of your life, no less—on three granola bars. Plus, to make matters even worse, as soon as they got just a morsel of what they wanted from him, they got him a pizza! His favorite Bulldog pizza!

"It's no wonder he gave a confession. The reinforcement was extraordinary. You all heard the testimony of Dr. Kay Robinson, a psychiatrist who specializes in confessions. I don't think you will forget the words she spoke when she looked at Ezekiel. I know I won't. She said, 'I'm telling you as a physician, and a human, that I would have sold my own children to get out of the room. Without food and sleep, we become irrational animals in small rooms.'

"If there were any justice in this world, the Duluth Police Department would be on trial today—along with Craig Kellerman. But sadly, life is not fair, and neither is justice. It's frustrating. But don't let that frustration lead you to disregard the truth.

"All right, I'm coming to the end of this unplanned argument. And ironically, I want to end with another item that Ms. Richards and I agree on. As she so eloquently stated, it is your job to give a voice to those who cannot speak for themselves. Yes, that is your job—and it's an awesome one at that. But I'll tell you what I think those voiceless people are saying to you. They are saying, 'Do not let our deaths be in vain. Do not convict the wrong person. We are worth more than that—we are worth the truth.'

"So thank you, members of the jury, for your time and attention. You have an incredible responsibility today. I am asking you to find Ezekiel Smith innocent of all the counts of first-degree murder and all the counts of burglary with a deadly weapon. I'm asking that because he simply wasn't there. I am also asking you to find Ezekiel Smith innocent of the manslaughter of Craig Kellerman. I'm asking that because it was self-defense.

"Now, if it pleases the court, the defense has concluded this trial."

Mr. Feirri picked up his torn papers from the floor and walked back to his place beside Zeke. Everyone was silent.

42

ZEKE'S LAST VERSION

Zeke liked his holding cell inside the Dakota County Jail in Hastings. For the past year, until he'd been transferred for the trial, he had been held at the St. Louis County Jail in Duluth. The people there had not been nearly as nice to him, and the food had been terrible. Things in Hastings were much better.

He hadn't been offered bail. But to be fair, Kurt Feirri hadn't fought very hard to get a judge to grant bail in the first place. Zeke had known he wouldn't be safe on his own and had agreed to wait things out in jail.

This was the first night in seven weeks that Zeke wasn't nervous for the next day. The case had gone to the jury, and he wouldn't see any of them until they had made a decision. He used to worry about every movement and every hair—he didn't want to do the slightest thing to make himself look guilty. He needed to appear like a nice guy who'd gotten caught up with a bad guy and made a coerced confession. He didn't need to worry about any of that now. *There's nothing I can do about anything right now. As hard as it is, I'm going to wait for the verdict. If it's innocent, I'll let myself be happy. If it's guilty, I'll let myself be worried. Prison won't be like either of the jails I've been in.*

Craig would be so proud of me tonight—I mean, he is very proud of me tonight. I followed his plan, and it's gone well. Any day now, they will say I'm not guilty, and I'll be free. I did it all for him, and he'll be with me the rest of my life, no matter if I meet someone new or not.

Sitting on his bed, Zeke looked over at a tiny ledge attached to the wall, made of cement blocks. His few personal items were on the ledge. He bent over to grab a stack of envelopes. *Gene's letters help to pass the time. He's no Craig, but he's been here for me this whole year. Gene knows how to make me feel good about myself. That's what I need right now.* Zeke had started receiving letters from Gene Hancke of Pine City, Minnesota, fairly soon after he was incarcerated. Gene, a fifty-two-year-old gay bachelor, believed fully in Zeke's innocence. They wrote each other often and had met several times, on opposite sides of the glass. *Gene's been at every day of the trial. He must really like me. Too bad I couldn't have put him on my official guest list to guarantee him a seat—my parents would have freaked. Gene probably gets to the courthouse before four each morning just to get a seat. It's sweet. He's no Craig. He certainly doesn't look like Craig. But he's there.*

Zeke was partway through a letter when he started to get tired. *I'm glad I'm tired. I was afraid I wouldn't be able to calm down tonight.* He put the letters back on the ledge and lay back on his pillow. He put his arms behind his head.

It was hard to listen to the Richards woman and her closing statement. It was hard because she got a fair amount of it right. But she's missing a lot of it too. Kurt was great—he ripped her to shreds. I know he had his speech prepared way before and memorized the whole thing. That's him. But his whole act of ripping up his pages was fun to watch—and I think it made a good point to the jury. All that money that my parents and their friends spent went to good use. I could see myself with Kurt. I tried, but he never went for it. Maybe I'll try again after a few months, when I'm not his client anymore. It's interesting that Richards got so much right just from the little evidence she had to piece together. Richards is a smarter person than Kurt, but Kurt is a much better lawyer.

Richards got Edy McCabe right, but that was expected since Edy was around for the whole burglary, and I didn't kill her. But in real life, she was a lot more difficult than what anyone thinks. I didn't even tell Craig how hard it was. He was around at the Kearneys', double-checking everything. With the McCabe woman, I had to keep looking around and checking on myself. And she just wouldn't stop screaming. God, she doesn't know how close she came to getting her head blown off. She was so shaky. I was afraid she'd have a heart attack when she was getting me the money. I wonder if I would have just left her there if she'd really had a heart attack. I guess I probably would have.

The old woman's eyes were weird. It wasn't like she was afraid of me. She didn't even have a sense of defiance. It was more like she just really wanted the whole thing to end as fast as it could. Maybe that's what saved her life? Any old woman like that who went to Dad's church had to be a real homophobic bitch, so I guess she owed me.

But Hank Neilson, now there was a real piece of shit. All that money he made by screwing over the workers in the iron ore mines, and all he had in the house was a lousy two hundred. I could have let him sleep—he didn't hear me when I crawled into his bedroom. But he just looked like an asshole. So I turned the light on and sent terror into his eyes. God, I loved seeing those eyes, until he started to talk back. There was no way I was letting him live. He didn't deserve to, especially after he called me a faggot. He didn't have any clue who I was—he didn't know I was gay. He must have just called anyone who argued with him a faggot. I wonder how many of the workers on the Iron Range got called a faggot by him because they argued when he screwed them over. As soon as he said that word, I knew what I had to do.

Shooting is so much messier than strangling. God, there was so much blood! So much! What a mess. I made sure I had everything and left with the lousy two hundred. He was lying there when I left. What a way to end a life—full of blood.

The Dockindorf woman really did sleep through the whole thing. God, there was so much crap in that house. And the smoke! I think I got cancer just walking into that place—I should sue her. What kind of nurse can she possibly be? I probably left some of Hank's blood in there, but how would anyone know? There's no way to scan for prints or DNA when it's floor-to-ceiling garbage in all corners.

Craig didn't seem too impressed when I got back that night. Maybe he was tired. I'm sure he realized how much I was doing so that the two of us could be together.

Was Lisa Sumner next? She must have been the first of the next night, because I went there before I got to Hendricks—I remember that for sure. She wasn't home—that was true. I could really get into that. Robbing a house when no one is there is kind of fun. You feel like you have all this space and time. And anything you do doesn't matter. Craig was right about the temptation to take things—it's so powerful, especially in an empty home. I could have taken so many things. But Craig always told me that taking anything except cash was too risky. He was right. What if I'd taken a piece of her jewelry and then they'd found it on me? I guess I could have said that Craig had given it to me, but as Craig always said, any physical item can tell a story through DNA and fingerprints.

Charles Hendricks was next. Holy God, that was bizarre. He had all that money, but I didn't find it exactly like I told Craig. I was in the house, looking for cash—for anything. I found the plastic box of cash. I was happy. But underneath the box of cash, I found a huge stack of real bad stuff, a whole pile of kids—young kids—in pornography. It creeped me out. I was going to take the money and the kid stuff. I knew that Craig wouldn't like it, but I wanted to get rid of it. So gross.

But then Hendricks woke up and came out of the bedroom. He scared the crap out of me. I didn't know if he'd called 911 or not. God, I was so worried because I didn't want Craig to be disappointed if I got caught. He started yelling, but then I yelled back. I told him that I'd seen the child porn. I told him that I was taking the cash and leaving. I said that he'd better get rid of his porn stuff before he called the police. Then I left.

I probably should have skipped the Carlson woman, or at least let it go until the next night. At that point I still thought there'd be a next night—damn Williams. I was going to save the candlestick for the last night because I knew it'd make a lot of forensic evidence. But I got surprised. Anna Carlson was in bed, and everything was going well. But then she suddenly recognized me. She said that she knew my voice from the church. She said that my parents were worried about me and that she would help me. Then she said that they all knew I was living with a bad man. I just couldn't listen to that. She wanted to take Craig away from me and me away from Craig. I had to shoot her in the head. I had to make her stop talking.

I should have run out of the house, but I heard that kid asking for his grandma. He was coming down the hall and asking for Grandma. I had the candlestick in the satchel and thought, What the hell? Might as well use it in case I don't have another chance. And I had that odd feeling that this kid was going to end up in Hendricks's gross porn. So I beat him to save him. Ms. Richards had that right. I beat him to death. But he must have been surrounded by family that was homophobic. He would have grown up to be a real asshole anyway. It's a good thing that he was there.

Thank God for the Duluth police. That confession tape played well—real well. I don't think even Craig thought that it would look that perfect. He'd be so proud of me. I dragged it out as long as I could in the station. I am really going to get away with all this—and like Craig said, I'm going to do it by telling the truth.

Craig didn't tell the truth at the end of his life—I know he didn't. He said that he wasn't even gay. That's not true. He was. How could he have done all that stuff with me if he wasn't gay? He loved me. But he said that so that I would kill him and have a plausible story to tell the police. He did this all for me—he had it all planned out. As soon as I killed Kearney, he started to plan all this out. And it worked—hopefully. We'll know soon.

Craig, whatever I do for the rest of my life, I owe it all to you.

Zeke turned over onto his stomach and held his pillow as if it were Craig. He fell asleep.

43

FIVE MINUTES OF FAME

When Zeke went to bed on the third night of jury deliberations, there was still no sign of a decision. In St. Louis County, he hadn't been allowed any sort of technology in his cell. But here in Dakota County, he was allowed a regular radio with headphones. He went to sleep nightly listening to a talk radio station. Often, someone was discussing the *State of Minnesota v. Ezekiel Smith*. Tonight, he heard the voice of his favorite of the commentators—a prosecutor who had worked in Minnesota's most populous county, Hennepin, for over forty years. She was a force to be reckoned with.

"I can't go anywhere right now without people asking me that," she said over the radio waves. "Which side is going to win because the jury is taking so long to reach a verdict? Well, I will tell all of you that the only thing you can tell about a long jury deliberation is that it's a long jury deliberation—that's it. Don't listen to the legal pundits. I've heard some of them say that more than three days means a guaranteed win for the prosecution, and I've heard others say the exact opposite. I am telling you, the only thing this means is that the jury is divided and has not made a decision. Either side can still win at this point.

"Now, we know that the jury has not asked to reexamine any of the testimony or to see any of the exhibits. We also know that they have not informed the judge that they are at an impasse and won't be able to decide. These are good signs. This means that the jury is very serious about doing its job.

"Others have asked me what I think of the two lead attorneys. Which one did a better job? Well, Ms. Richards, in my opinion, made a crucial mistake. I actually know her. She's very bright—one of the most intelligent people I know in the legal business. But maybe her intelligence worked against her in this case. Here's the mistake: I think it wasn't a great idea to focus so much on evidence when so much of the evidence is missing. Now you might not like hearing that from me. You might want Ezekiel Smith to be locked away forever. And maybe I do too. But all I am saying is that there is missing evidence. I think Richards made a mistake spending so much time on it.

"But to her favor, she did a great job of laying out a story. She gave the jury a sequence of events that possibly could have occurred. Juries need to be able to visualize a linear story that makes sense—Richards gave that to them.

"I also think that Richards made an enormous mistake when she called the sixth-grade teacher. The sixth-grade teacher was asked to describe Ezekiel's obsession with Glensheen. Richards was trying to show that Ezekiel was apt to kill someone with a candlestick because he was obsessed with the Glensheen murders—one of which also occurred with a candlestick. However, Richards had to have known that the defense team was just going to ask the teacher if she'd had other students obsessed with Glensheen. When the teacher answered yes, it made the prosecution look weak. If I'm on the jury, I'm thinking, 'Seriously? That's all they have to connect the candlestick to Ezekiel instead of Craig Kellerman?' It would have been much better to just leave the teacher up in Duluth.

"Now Mr. Feirri is a force—there is no doubt about that. He was right to go after Richards's obsession with the evidence in her closing statement. But I don't think for a second he tore up his speech and made up his whole statement on the spot. This was a well-planned speech, and I think it went off very well. He did his job. He pointed out all the holes in the prosecution's case, and he provided a story that makes sense: that Craig Kellerman was the real killer. I've said it many times—the defense must give the jury an alternate story that makes sense and takes away all blame from the defendant. I think that Feirri mostly accomplished that.

"However, Feirri dropped the ball with one aspect. And I have to tell you, if I'm on the jury, this aspect of the case is really going to bother me. If Ezekiel Smith was not the second burglar at the Kearney house in Hibbing, then who was? Feirri should have given us a name, or at least a plausible identity. Maybe it was another guy who worked at the restaurant? Maybe it was a college friend? Maybe it was some gay guy that Craig met in a bar? Come on, Feirri, you needed to give us a second person to think about, a specific person. In my mind, without another possibility, I'm thinking that Ezekiel had to have been at the Kearney house with Kellerman.

"Now let's talk about that confession. Was it coerced? Was it authentic? If I'm on the jury, I'm thinking that it's real. He admitted to the crimes and seemed to know the details that filled in the blanks. Now I do understand how some people think that the police fed him those details, or at least flushed them out for him. But the story he told was there, and I'm fairly inclined to believe it.

"So I guess I'm saying that it's anyone's game at this point. What do I personally think? How would I, with all my experience, vote? Well, I think he's guilty on all counts. There's enough evidence for my comfort, and I've never been one to believe in Stockholm syndrome. But I'm not on the jury. So we'll have to wait and see.

"And here is one last thought that you should engrave on your brain. If you're in trouble, if you're in a police station, don't say anything! You don't have to talk at all—so many people think that you have to talk to the police. You don't. Get a lawyer. You won't look guilty. The only thing you should ever tell the police, no matter how small the circumstances, is 'I want a lawyer.' Don't say, 'I need a lawyer.' Say, 'I want a lawyer.' That's it."

Huh. I guess I'm glad she's not on the jury. But someone as educated as her would never be on a jury anyway. Kurt told me, 'We want dumb people who think they're smart.' She'd never make it on a jury.

Zeke hugged his Craig pillow and went to sleep for the third night of no decision.

44

THE BAKER'S DOZEN

The word came at 8:30 a.m. that next morning: the jury was back. They'd reached a verdict. Up to this point, there had always been a chance of being found not guilty, found guilty, or having a mistrial. *Well, a mistrial is out of the question now. I'm left with just the other two options: guilty or not guilty.*

Zeke's courtroom clothes were brought to his cell. Mr. Feirri arrived and waited for him to change. Then the attorney entered the cell and sat with Zeke for a few minutes.

"So, Zeke," Kurt said, "you ready for this?"

"Yep. I'm ready to get this over with."

"Okay, so let's talk. You know that there are two possibilities. I'm going to ask that, whichever one it is, you stay calm and not say anything. Remember, they will read each count separately. So it's important not to react until they complete all of them. But I don't think you'll have a problem with that. I know you well enough by now."

"Yeah, it won't be a problem. I'll just look ahead."

"Good. If it's guilty, on any of the counts, then you'll be taken away and brought back here until sentencing. Depending on which of the counts is guilty, we'll make a plan to proceed. If you're innocent of all the counts, then you'll just go ahead with your plan to get away from the media for a while. Do you still have your plans in place?"

"Yes, the same plan I went over with you."

"Did you double-check that everyone knows what to do and where to go? We really need to get you away from the courthouse as quickly as we can."

"Yep. I just checked this morning. Everything is ready."

"Okay. Your parents are going to hate it. Do they know anything about it?"

"Nope."

"That's probably good, but it will be important to let them know that you're not going with them and then get out of the courtroom with the escort. I'll contact you in a day or so. Just remember, this is not the time for emotion. That can come later."

"I understand."

The courtroom was silent. All the players were in their places, including the attorneys, Zeke, and the entire Smith family. Every seat had been taken. The families of the victims were all there. Zeke avoided their horrified stares, but he'd gotten used to doing that over the past seven weeks.

Zeke didn't look for Gene Hancke, his new boyfriend. It wasn't part of the plan for Gene to be inside the courtroom that day. There were reporters filling up the back rows. Minnesota did not allow cameras in courtrooms, and Zeke saw the same two sketch artists who had been there for the whole trial. They were both already working quickly. *That's the dumbest thing in here. They should just allow a camera. Those sketch artists don't make anyone look the way they really do.*

The judge was in place, and the jury was brought in. Zeke looked at them. Some of them looked back at him. That made him uncomfortable, so he decided to stare at a flag of Minnesota that was directly in front of him. Kurt Feirri put his arm around him, squeezed, and then released him.

After a few formalities that to Zeke seemed to last an eternity, the judge was ready for the verdicts. "On the count of burglary at the

Kearney residence in Hibbing, Minnesota, how do you find?" the judge asked the jury foreperson.

"Not guilty."

Oh yes, this is a very good sign. If I wasn't there for burglary, then they know I wasn't there for murder.

"On the count of the first-degree murder of Daniel Kearney, how do you find?"

"Not guilty."

"On the count of the burglary of Edy McCabe, how do you find?"

"Not guilty."

It's not guilty again. And again. Hank Neilson, Sarah Dockindorf— not guilty. Lisa Sumner and the pedophile Hendricks—not guilty. Not guilty on all of the burglaries. Not guilty of the murders of Anna Carlson and her grandson Tucker. They think Craig did it all. Thank you, Craig. God, I really love you. But the last one might be tricky.

"And finally, on the count of the manslaughter of Craig Kellerman, how do you find?"

"Not guilty."

They believed it all. I was a captive with Stockholm syndrome. I killed Craig in self-defense. I'll be free.

Kurt put his arm around Zeke and squeezed hard. Zeke breathed deeply and hugged him back. There was a lot of noise in the room, but Zeke couldn't comprehend any of it. He saw the face of Marilyn Richards, the St. Louis County prosecutor. She looked depressed and tired. He wanted, badly, to look at the jury, but he didn't. *Don't look at them. It might be like a jinx. Just don't look at them—don't give them a sign that they made the wrong decision. We did it, Craig! We did it! We got away with murder by telling the truth.*

He looked for the slightest second at the rows of people sitting behind the prosecution's table. They were crying. Some were making loud sounds. *Don't pay attention to them. They don't know anything.*

Kurt signaled for one of the sheriff's deputies to come over. "We need to take him to the holding room right away," the attorney said.

Before Zeke could take another look around the courtroom, the deputy grabbed him, and he was quickly taken through a door.

45

ANOTHER LEOPOLD AND ANOTHER LOEB

There was a flurry of activity inside the holding room. Kurt could not stop beaming and proudly patting Zeke on the back.

He should be patting me on the back. I've just made his entire career. He'll be famous and make a ton of money. It's a good thing my parents were able to afford him while they could.

Pastor and Mrs. Smith were allowed into the room by a deputy. They both ran over to their son and threw their arms around him.

"I knew it," Mrs. Smith said through tears. "I knew that you did not do these things. You were led astray by Satan, and now Jesus Christ, your Lord and savior, has led you back to the light."

"Yes, so true," Pastor Smith agreed. "We will have a feast at our church that will be fit for the prodigal son. I will kill the fatted calf!" He laughed loudly.

I can't stand it. I'd rather go to prison than be with these people again. Who talks like that? God, Craig, I really miss you.

"Mr. Feirri," a deputy interrupted, "we really need to get him out of here. There's a lot of media out there. His ride is ready, right by the loading dock door."

"What ride?" Pastor Smith asked.

"He's being taken to an undisclosed location," Kurt Feirri replied. "At least until things calm down."

"Where?" Mrs. Smith asked.

"My job is done," said Feirri. "That's up to Zeke to tell you."

"Ezekiel? Son?" Pastor Smith said.

"Yeah," said Zeke, "I'm going with a friend for a bit. Maybe longer."

"We need to go," said the deputy as he grabbed Zeke by the arm and led him out of the room.

Zeke could hear his parents yelling at Feirri all down the hallway that led to a rear loading dock of the courthouse. *I'll never have to see them again. But I've said that before.*

The deputy opened a door aside a loading ramp. In the dock, the black Mercedes looked rather small to Zeke. But it was his Mercedes. Inside, he saw Gene Hancke behind the wheel. Zeke didn't say a word to the deputy. He didn't even bother to ask about any of his stuff from his cell. *Kurt will get anything that's mine and get it to me. If he doesn't, no big loss.*

Zeke got into the passenger seat and closed the door. Gene bent over and kissed him on the cheek.

"I've waited so long to be able to touch you," Gene said. "I'm so happy for you and for me. I just—oh, I just want to grab you right now. But we have to go. It's getting crazy outside. There are people everywhere, and they told me just to get out of here as soon as possible."

Gene backed the car down the ramp and turned it around in a large concrete parking area. They waited for a guard to open a large garage door, and then they drove quickly off of the Dakota County Courthouse property.

Zeke kept looking forward. *You can be done thinking about the trial now.*

"I've got everything ready for you at home," Gene said. "The security system is up—so no need to worry about anything. You're safe with me. Your bedroom and bathroom are all set."

"Thanks for everything, Gene," Zeke said. "I don't know what I'd do without you."

He looked a lot handsomer through glass. But oh well. A car and a bedroom? I can deal with this. And I've been working out every day for the last year. He's going to love my body. That will be good for me. I can use that to my advantage.

46

THEY HAVE THE
FINAL WORD

Zeke woke up in his very own bedroom inside Gene's house. They'd arrived at the home early in the afternoon, and Zeke had wanted to take a nap. *God, it feels so good to sleep in an actual bed for once. And this house is amazing.* Gene owned a large new home on the shore of Pokegama Lake, and Zeke's bedroom contained large floor-to-ceiling windows overlooking the water. He had appreciated the view before falling asleep.

Gene also had given Zeke a brand-new phone. Zeke picked it up to check the time. *God, it's after seven already. I've slept a long time. I'm hungry, and something smells really good. He's probably letting me sleep and keeping dinner warm. Gene is very sweet. But I might be able to catch the seven o'clock show I love and see if she's talking about my case.*

Zeke used his new smartphone to navigate to the radio station that he'd listened to while he was incarcerated. He turned the volume up but kept it low enough that Gene wouldn't realize he was awake. *Oh good, I didn't miss it. And she is talking about me! This should be good.*

The commentator and former Hennepin County attorney said,

"Like I said before, you can't tell which way a jury is going to go just by how long they take to deliberate. But anyway, let's get to the main part of the show. I have, in the studio with me, two of the jurors from the Ezekiel Smith trial. Now to protect them, we're not going to say their names. I'll refer to them as Juror 1 and Juror 2. So, Juror 1, let's start with you. Just so that the listeners know, can you tell me how old you are and where in Dakota County you live?"

"Sure," replied a female voice. "I'm forty-seven, and I live in Apple Valley."

"And without giving up too much personal information," said the commentator, "do you work?"

"Yes, I'm a teacher."

"Okay, great. So tell us, did you think that Ezekiel was innocent right from the start of deliberations, or did you change your mind?"

"Well," said Juror 1, "I'd pretty much thought he was innocent since the trial itself ended. I guess I never wavered from that."

"And why was that? Why do you think he didn't commit the crimes?"

"Well, for me it all comes down to the two men. During the whole trial, I was looking at Craig Kellerman and Ezekiel Smith. We know that only one of them did the crimes in Duluth. I guess, for me, I needed to make a decision as to which one of them did the crimes. It just doesn't make sense to me that Ezekiel Smith, right out of high school, could do those things. But it does make sense that Craig Kellerman would do them."

"And what about some of the evidence that pointed to Ezekiel's guilt? All the victims being from his father's church roster, the fingerprints on the ketamine syringe, the handcuff wounds on Craig's wrist—what about that evidence?"

"Well, all of that stuff was explained in the trial. Craig Kellerman would have had access to the church directory, or whatever it was. And Craig was also into some really ... ah ... pushing-it stuff. I mean, when it came to sex. So the fingerprints and the handcuffs don't bother me. And like the defense attorney said, if Ezekiel had killed him earlier in the day, why use an apron when there were so many other weapons in the house?"

"So, Juror 1, do you believe that Ezekiel Smith was a victim of Stockholm syndrome? Because I think that in order to vote not guilty, you have to believe that."

"Yes, I do. I absolutely believe that Ezekiel Smith was a prisoner in that home. Like I said, I'm a teacher. This means that I have a lot of training in students and their emotional needs. And we do get training on gay students and how they grow up. I think it was so easy for Craig Kellerman to get inside of Ezekiel's head. I really feel terrible for him—Ezekiel, I mean. He grew up being really restricted and was easily taken in by the first guy who showed him some affection. So yeah, I do believe that Ezekiel was a victim of Stockholm syndrome and was a prisoner in that house."

"And lastly, Juror 1," the commentator continued, "what do you think of the confession? Was it coerced?"

"Oh, absolutely! As a teacher, I know how these things works. I could tell without any doubt that Ezekiel was manipulated into that confession. I mean, come on—he was tired and hungry. It went on for hours. I felt so terrible for him. I saw a lot of my students in him, and I know that many of them would have done the same thing. I have a lot of background on this kind of thing. I really believe that any of us would have confessed in that situation."

"Okay, thank you. So let's go to Juror 2," said the commentator. "Can you tell us how old you are and where you live?"

"I'm seventy-two," said a male voice, "and I live in a small town in the rural part of Dakota County. I don't want to say which one."

"No problem. Do you work?"

"I'm a retired postal carrier."

"So did you always feel that Ezekiel Smith was not guilty?"

"No, I really didn't," Juror 2 replied. "I was the last holdout during the deliberations. I went into the deliberation thinking that he was guilty."

"First, tell us why you thought he was guilty," said the commentator.

"I didn't buy the whole prisoner deal. The neighbors all said that Ezekiel seemed happy to be living with Craig. They saw the two of them together all the time. And many people saw them running together. There had to have been a chance for Ezekiel to escape. I—"

"So you don't believe in Stockholm syndrome?"

"Not really. No. I think that a person can always change their circumstance if they want. Now if he'd been tied up for a whole year, and if nobody had ever seen him outside, then that would have been a different story."

"Why did you change your mind? It seems like you still don't believe he was a prisoner."

"I don't—I don't think that Ezekiel was a prisoner at all. And I want to tell you that I voted not guilty. I didn't vote innocent. To me, there is a big difference. See, I still think that there is a real chance that Ezekiel Smith killed those people and robbed those homes. But I had to keep an open mind—and the longer we talked in the jury room, the more I realized that there was a lot of reasonable doubt. So even though I may still be inclined to believe that he did the crimes, there is too much doubt. If you're going to lock someone up for the rest of their life—especially someone as young as Ezekiel Smith— then you really want to make sure that it's beyond reasonable doubt."

"And you felt that there were enough holes in the prosecution's case?"

"Yes. See, we were up really late last night—that's why they didn't announce until this morning. And it was in that last hour—I was still a holdout for guilty—that I realized I had to recognize that Craig Kellerman could have done the murders. So that's it. He could have. But still, so could have Ezekiel Smith."

"And the confession—forced or real?"

"Well, I have to say that I think it was real. I believe that nobody is ever going to say they did something that they didn't do. I know that I wouldn't, no matter how tired or hungry I was. I just wouldn't."

"Yet you voted not guilty. So in the end, you must have disregarded the confession."

"Well, I wouldn't say that I disregarded it. Nope, I think it's still important. And like I said, I think there is a good chance that he's guilty. But there's a chance that he's not. And in this particular case—others on the jury discussed it a lot with me—a young person might just confess to something they didn't do."

"So did you send a guilty man back into the community?"

"Maybe," Juror 2 replied. "Maybe. I just don't know. But you see, that's it—I'm not really sure that he is guilty. It's not a perfect system, but it's the system we have. Yep, we might have let a guilty person go free. But I guess that's better than locking up an innocent person for the rest of his life."

"And you, Juror 1—did you send a guilty man back into the community?"

"Absolutely not," she replied. "I am convinced he's innocent. And all my teaching experience and training reinforce my decision. I will sleep well tonight."

"Well, let's leave it at that and go to a break. When we return, we'll be talking by phone with the widow of Dan Kearney, the man who was murdered in Hibbing. She was one of the pivotal witnesses for the prosecution in the case of Ezekiel Smith and will probably offer a very different opinion of the verdict than what we've talked about so far."

Zeke turned off the radio stream on his phone. *Who wants to listen to that? Mrs. Kearney is not on my side. What a lucky break for me that she was caught saying homophobic things! Let's see what Gene's got going for food.*

Zeke looked out onto the darkness that was Pokegama Lake. From the large dining room table, he could see through the living room and out a set of enormous two-story windows. He could see lights way out in the distance.

"Are those lights coming from the other side of the lake?" Zeke asked.

"Yep," said Gene. "So we have a lot of privacy here. You don't need to worry about a thing."

"Do you have a boat?"

"Yes, we have a boat. What's the point of living on a lake if you don't have a boat?"

This is going to be a good life. "So, Gene," Zeke said, "I want to go to Hibbing tomorrow—you know, after I get a good night's sleep."

"Hibbing? Seriously?"

"Yeah, I want to visit Craig's grave. And then I want to go to Sauk Centre sometime and see Craig's vase. That's what it will always be to me—not Sinclair Lewis's urn, but Craig's vase where we put our flowers. I don't even know where Sauk Centre is."

"I don't think either of those places would be good for you right now," Gene said.

"You're probably right. I just thought that if we both got a good night of sleep together in your bed, then we might be ready for a road trip tomorrow. But you're right. We should play it safe and probably sleep in separate rooms—take it slow for a while."

"Then again," Gene said, "you are free and clear. It's nobody's business if you are with another man already. If you want to go to Hibbing and Sauk Centre, then Hibbing and Sauk Centre it is."

"Thanks. You're the best," Zeke said robotically.

CONCLUSION

It was now up to Judge John R. Caverly to determine whether Leopold and Loeb would be given the death sentence for the killing of fourteen-year-old Bobby Franks in 1924. He had to consider Clarence Darrow's twelve-hour speech as well as the testimony of over one hundred experts on either side of the issue. One of the experts had blamed Leopold and Loeb's dysfunctional endocrine glands for the crime.

The judge deliberated for twelve days. On September 10, 1924, he sided with Clarence Darrow. The men were sentenced to life in prison, plus ninety-nine years.

On January 28, 1936, Richard Loeb, the man obsessed with committing the perfect crime, was stabbed over fifty times with a razor in a prison shower. James Day, another inmate, stated that Loeb had been trying to rape him, and he had no choice but to kill him. The prison homicide of Richard Loeb went to trial. During the trial, several other inmates and the prison's Catholic priest testified that Loeb was not homosexual and never would have wanted to have sex with James Day. It was James Day, they claimed, who was homosexual and wanted to have sex with Loeb. When Loeb refused, Day killed him. However, the jury believed James Day's story, and he was acquitted of the charge of murder.

Nathan Leopold, the gay man who was deeply in love with Loeb, reorganized the prison library. In 1944, he volunteered to be inoculated with malaria so that scientists could study the impact of an experimental malaria vaccine. That act made him eligible for parole, despite his long sentence. In March 1958, after serving thirty-three years for the murder of Bobby Franks, Nathan Leopold was released from prison. He moved to Puerto Rico and died there of diabetes at the age of sixty-six in 1971.

The adequacy of Leopold and Loeb's sentence continues to be debated today. Clarence Darrow's use of childhood situational trauma to explain later psychosis remains a valid defense. Juries still face the task of deciding whether the explanation should also be an excuse.

Was the Evil Queen simply driven by envy in her desire to be the fairest of them all? Maybe the true villains were her parents, her grandparents, or the guy who made the mirror.

Was the Big Bad Wolf a homicidal maniac who destroyed homes in his quest for blood? Or did he just have really bad allergies? In any case, the reason for his behavior didn't matter much to the pigs.

9 781480 898813